Welcome to Land of Fright™

Land of Fright™ is a world of spine-tingling short horror stories filled with the strange, the eerie, and the weird. The **Land of Fright™** series encompasses the vast expanse of time and space. You will visit the world of the Past in Ancient Rome, Medieval England, the old West, World War II, and other eras yet to be explored. You will find many tales that exist right here in the Present, tales filled with modern lives that have taken a turn down a darker path. You will travel into the Future to tour strange new worlds and interact with alien societies, or to just take a disturbing peek at what tomorrow may bring.

Each **Land of Fright™** story exists in its own territory (which we like to call a **terrorstory**.) These terrorstories can be visited in any order you choose. Some of the story realms you visit will intrigue you. Some of them may unsettle you. Some of them may even titillate and amuse you. We hope many of them will give you delicious chills along your journey. And there are many new uncharted realms yet to be mapped, so keep checking back for new discoveries.

First, we need to check your ID. **Land of Fright™** is intended for mature audiences. You will experience adult language, graphic violence, and some explicit sex. Ready to enter? Good. We'll take that ticket now. **Land of Fright™** awaits. You can pass through the dark gates and—Step Into Fear!

Readers Love Land of Fright™!

"This is the first story I've read by this author and it blew me away! A gripping tale that kept me wondering until the end. Images from this will, I fear, haunt me at unexpected moments for many months to come. Readers, be warned! :)" – Amazon review for **Dung Beetles (Land of Fright™ #27 – in Collection III)**

"Some truly original stories. At last, a great collection of unique and different stories. Whilst this is billed as horror, the author managed to steer away from senseless violence and gratuitous gore and instead with artful story telling inspires you to use your own imagination. A great collection. Already looking for other collections... especially loved Kill the Queen (God Save the Queen)." – Amazon UK review for **Land of Fright™ Collection I**

"This was a great story. Even though it was short I still connected with the main character and was rooting for her. Once I read the twist I cheered her on. This was an enjoyable short story." – Amazon review for **Snowflakes (Land of Fright™ #3 – in Collection I)**

"Love the freaky tales from the Land of Fright. This one is particularly nasty and dark. A tale of double revenge unfolds in a graveyard where a perceived business betrayal causes the perceiver to enact an insidious plan to impose the ultimate suffering on his partner. The suffering takes an unexpected turn that I did not see coming." – Amazon review for **Cemetery Dance (Land of Fright™ #49 – in Collection V)**

"I absolutely loved the heck out of this story. The whole story was bizarre, and the end? Well, it was perfect!" – Amazon review for **The Throw-Aways (Land of Fright™ #31 – in Collection IV)**

"I like the idea of a malevolent dimension that finds a way to reach into our world… this was an entertaining read and can be read at lunch or as a palate cleanser between longer stories." – Amazon review for **Sparklers (Land of Fright™ #15 – in Collection II)**

"I enjoyed this quite a bit, but then I enjoy anything set in Pompeii. A horror story is a first, though, and well done. I'm become a fan of the author and so far have enjoyed several of his stories." – Amazon review for **Ghosts of Pompeii (Land of Fright™ #14 – in Collection II)**

"Fantastic science fiction short that has a surprising plot twist, great aliens, cool future tech and occurs in a remote lived-in future mining colony on a distant planet. This short hit all the marks I look for in science fiction stories. The alien creatures are truly alien and attack with a mindless ruthlessness. The desperate colonists defend themselves in a uniquely futuristic way. This work nails the art of the short story. Recommended." – Amazon review for **Out of Ink (Land of Fright™ #26 – in Collection III)**

"I am a fan of the Land of Fright series and have found the horror found in the stories diverse and delightfully bizarre. This tale amp's up the gritty to 11. The barbarian warrior king in this short story is a well written, fearsome, crude and believable beast of a man. This story is not for those offended by sex or violence. I was immersed and found it great escapism, exactly what I look for in recreational reading."- Amazon review for **The King Who Owned The World (Land of Fright™ #50 – in Collection V)**

"Another great story; I've become a fan of Mr. O'Donnell. Please keep them coming…" – Amazon review for **Sands of the Colosseum (Land of Fright™ #18 – in Collection II)**

"Perfect bite size weirdness. Land of Fright does it again with this Zone like short that has two creative plot twists that really caught me off guard. I know comparing this type of work to the Twilight Zone is overdone but it really is a high compliment that denotes original, well conceived and delightfully weird short fiction. Recommended." – Amazon review for **Flipbook (Land of Fright™ #19 – in Collection II)**

"An enjoyable story; refreshingly told from the point of view of the cat...definitely good suspense." – Amazon review for **Pharaoh's Cat (Land of Fright™ #30 – in Collection III)**

"A fun thrill-ride into the Mexican jungle, and another great Land of Fright tale. Not enough people have written horror stories or novels about Aztec sacrifices." -Amazon review for **Virgin Sacrifice (Land of Fright™ #42 – in Collection V)**

"This short has a cool premise and was very effective at quickly transporting me to the sands of the coliseum in ancient Rome. The images of dead and dying gladiators are detailed and vivid. There is a malevolent force that very much likes its job and is not about to give it up, ever. Recommended." – Amazon review for **Hammer of Charon (Land of Fright™ #29 - in Collection III)**

"The thing I like about the Land of Fright series of short stories is that they are so diverse yet share a common weird, unusual and original vibe. From horror to science fiction they are all powerful despite of their brevity. Another great addition to the Land of Fright festival of the odd." - Amazon review for **Snowflakes (Land of Fright™ #3 – in Collection I)**

Land of Fright™

Collection III

JACK O'DONNELL

DEDICATION

To all the screenwriters, directors, producers, actors, and everyone else involved in the production of all the great movies and TV shows I grew up with. Thanks for all the great entertainment.

LAND OF FRIGHT™
COLLECTION III
CONTENTS

TERRORSTORY #21
THE PROSPECTOR

"The occurrence of gold in large quantities in a district hitherto little visited by civilized man, and only known by the accounts of a few travelers, has naturally produced great excitement in the public mind and much anxiety as to the possible results."

- From The Gold-Seekers Manual by David T. Ansted, M.A. F.R.S.

It was another severed hand. Jeremiah Greenwall shook the steel prospecting pan he held, sending more of the loose bits of dirt through the tiny mesh. He was in his mid-thirties, his skin deeply tanned and weathered from years of exposure to the elements. An inordinate amount of dark hair covered his arms and his neck. He had short black hair, a flat pug nose, and a deep cleft in his upper lip that showed a few of his upper teeth at all times whether he smiled or not. He was not a man prone to smiling.

Jeremiah stared at the object in his pan, then shook the pan some more in a circular motion, clearing away more of the mud and pebbles, revealing more fingers. Another damn hand. He glanced over at the first hand he had found. The severed appendage was drying in the sunlight on the rock where he had placed it. He had found the first severed hand a few minutes ago. When he first plucked the severed appendage out of the water, he had immediately considered just dumping it back into the stream, but something made him refrain from acting on that impulse. Something inside him urged him to keep it, so he had set the hand down on the rock to dry in the sun and had resumed panning for what he was really after.

Gold.

Jeremiah stared down at the severed hand in his pan. It reminded him of a big fat pale spider with too few legs. A fat bald spider. Again, he thought about just tossing the appendage back into the stream, but something urged him to keep this one as well.

He shuffled through the water of the fast moving stream, his gimp right leg giving his movement an odd loping motion. Jeremiah had come to the San Francisco area in 1849 to partake in the greatest gold rush the world had ever seen. He had found a few nuggets that first year that helped him get by and brought him enough money to buy supplies to keep him going into 1850. He even had earned enough to purchase the steel pan from Jonah, the blacksmith in town, to replace the crude panning dish he had carved out of a block of wood.

Jeremiah stared at the severed hand. He surely hadn't expected to find this. He reached the bank of the stream and set the second severed hand down next to the first. Who was the poor fellow? Did the Indians get to him? Jeremiah had heard stories of some savages killing a prospector and his brother, but that was months ago and in an area not really close to where he was prospecting. Still, he knew there were some Indians in his area. He looked up and glanced around, but saw nothing but the soft slope of the bank, the light brush, and the thick trees beyond.

From what he had heard, the savages spent most of their time hunting the huge herds of deer that roamed the area. He had seen a group of about thirty of those animals just the other day. They were magnificent creatures with their smooth brown hides and their massive tree-branch-size antlers; he could've sworn some of the stags he had seen had antlers that alone were four feet tall. Maybe another prospector had killed a deer for meat and the Indians had killed him for taking their game. From what he had heard, the savages didn't take kindly to all these new people roaming about their sacred lands, especially if they took their game. Jeremiah was very careful to be respectful of the lands he prospected; he didn't kill any game and only bought his food from Hayman's Market in town.

Jeremiah glanced up the stream, wondering where the severed hands had come from. The cold water flowed towards him, careening off boulders, swirling around rocks. He knew Roarke, Filligan, and Jacobson were panning a few hundred yards up around the bend, but there was no one else visible in the secluded spot he had claimed. Jeremiah scowled at the thought of the three men. They had kicked him off his prior claim and forced him to move downstream to the spot he was in now. They had shown him some piece of paper with a judge's order on it that countered his original claim. He knew it was a bunch of bull, but he didn't have any means to fight them. He had tucked his tail between his legs and moved downstream. He wondered how long it would be before some other assholes pushed him out of this spot. His claim was valid, but he knew that didn't mean much out here in the wilds of California. Especially since he was alone and had no one to fight for him.

Something brushed against his leg and Jeremiah glanced down to see a dark mass lodged against the rocks near the shore. What in tarnation? He set his pan down and reached into the cold water. By all that's holy. It's an arm. A severed arm. He raised the arm up out of the water. There was part of a shoulder, an elbow and a forearm, but no hand. He glanced down at the hands sitting on the nearby rock. Was it all part of the same person? He set the severed arm down next to the hands.

And nearly leaped out of his skin when the hand moved. It slid along the rock to rejoin itself to the arm it belonged to, like a magnet being drawn to another magnet.

Jeremiah could only stare with eyes as big as harvest moons. His breath came in and out with quick and short shrill whistles through the gap in his teeth.

≈⊙≈

Jeremiah stood in his small one-room cabin, staring down at the two arms on his table. A mattress rested on a low bed frame in the far corner of the room. A small wood-burning stove was positioned in another corner, situated near the door he had made out of timber he had felled with his axe. The axe rested against the wall near the stove. The air was cool this time of year, but not cold, so he didn't feel a need to be burning a fire these days. A candle burned on a nearby cracked plate, casting flickering light over the severed limbs. Jeremiah had found the second arm in the stream a few minutes after finding the first. He had set the arm down near the second hand and it had done the same thing as the first arm had done - it rejoined itself with its hand. Just like that. The second hand had scooted along the top of the rock and just attached itself to its arm.

He had tried to tug the hands away from the arms, but he couldn't budge them. It was as if the hands had never been severed from their arms. He could see the ghost of a seam where they were rejoined, but he could not pull them apart no matter how hard he tried. It was as if they were melded back together.

Jeremiah stared at the hands as the candle's light licked at the flesh with its flickering tongue of shadow. Now that he had studied them a bit more closely, the hands seemed narrow and small, the fingers thinner than his own. The arms were slender, too. Muscular, but slender. Were they a woman's arms? He had a strong feeling that they were. Who was she? All of the women he had seen around the camps and in town were prostitutes. He had heard talk of some female prospectors, but he had never actually seen one himself. They were supposedly working the waters far upstream, but he had taken those stories to be fanciful rumors that warmed a lonely man's bed at night.

Maybe a mountain lion got at her? Jeremiah immediately dismissed that thought. The mountain lion wouldn't have just sliced her limbs off; it would surely have eaten her up, too. He shook his head. No, this looked like it was done by human hands. The cuts were far too precise to have come from animal teeth or claws. She must have really done something to end up like this, he thought. Done something real bad.

He stared at one of the slender hands. Jeremiah pictured the woman they belonged to. She had soft blonde hair. Bright blue eyes. A happy, easy smile. She had an ample chest, too. Big breasts he could feel when he hugged her tight against him. He felt a stirring in his loins. You'd better stop, Jeremiah. Stop before it's too late. But he knew it was already too late. There was no stopping the remedy to the months of loneliness. Months? Heck, years. Hell no. Not even years. His whole damn life was just an empty blur of loneliness.

He stared at the slender fingers. They had looked as wrinkled as a prune when he pulled them out of the water, but now they looked smooth and soft. They even had a pinkish hue to them. A soft, healthy sheen. He wondered how they would feel on him.

Jeremiah reached out and touched one of the fingers. It felt oddly warm. He stroked the finger, moving his hand slowly across it. He gently grabbed a finger and curled it. It remained in the position he put it in. He moved another finger and it remained curled. He wondered how they would feel down there.

He grabbed the arm and picked it up. The flesh of

the arm was warm in his hand. He knew that shouldn't have been possible, yet it was. He turned the arm this way and that, studying it. He turned it around so the hand was facing down away from him, and slowly lowered it, bringing it against his body. He rubbed the hand over his crotch. His manhood lengthened and hardened immediately. He rubbed the hand over his stiffness. Then quickly bolted upright, dropping the hand in a panic.

Jeremiah stared with wide eyes at the severed arm on the floor as the fingers on the hand moved. They quickly became still and he wondered if he had just imagined their movement. No, he had seen the slender fingers move. He was sure of it. And he had felt them. He had felt the fingers move on his body.

He continued to stare for a long moment. The fingers hadn't hurt him. They had just scared him. An undeniable stirring in his loins prompted him to reach for the arm. He hesitated for a moment, but then picked the arm up and looked at it. The fingers were still. Don't do it, Jeremiah. Don't be a fool. You just plucked that out of the stream. That's a dead woman's hand. That just ain't right.

He loosened the cord holding up his pants and slid the hand underneath the fabric. The fingers moved. They gripped him, and for a moment Jeremiah felt a rising panic. But when they started to stroke him with feathery smoothness, the tension in his face drained away.

<hr />

Jeremiah stood still, staring at a rough sketch of a woman pinned to the wall. He was in Hayman's

Market, the only general store for miles around. He needed a few supplies, some food, some soap, and a new shirt because the one he was wearing was so ragged it was about to fall off his shoulders. Barrels of foodstuffs, digging tools, clothing, boots, and other items filled the aisles and shelves. Jeremiah stared at the bold black letters written under the black and white drawing of the woman's face: **WANTED FOR MURDER. $500 REWARD.**

Jeremiah heard footsteps and turned to see Hayman, the store owner, stepping up to stand next to him. Hayman was a reedy, tall man with short black hair and a long, hooked nose. "Don't worry about her none," Hayman said.

Jeremiah turned back to study the sketch for a moment. The woman had slightly raised cheekbones, a delicate nose. She was rather pretty, he thought. Except for the cruel smirk on her lips.

Hayman wiped his hands on his apron, then reached up to the sketch and took it down from the wall. "They caught her last week and chopped her up with her own axe. Tossed her into the river. I been meaning to take this down, just keep forgetting." Hayman crumbled the sketch in his hands and tossed it into a nearby waste bin.

"What she do?" Jeremiah asked.

"Butchered half a dozen men with her axe before they stopped her. She just went crazy trying to steal their gold."

"Was she one of them ladies?"

Hayman shook his head. "No, she wasn't no lady of love, if that's what you mean. She was a prospector." He shook his head again. "Ain't got no place panning out here with the men. Ain't got no place."

Jeremiah stared at the empty spot on the wall where the sketch had been, then glanced at the crushed up paper in the garbage. Was that her? Was that his woman? He reached down for the piece of paper, but stopped when he heard a loud commotion coming from the store's entrance. He rose up and turned. A dark shadow of fear crossed Jeremiah's features.

Henry Crawker and Samuel Lourdis entered the store.

Crawker was a big son of a bitch. He had dark skin and long hair that hung halfway down his back. Jeremiah thought he must have fancied himself as an Indian warrior or something. Crawker even carried a tomahawk in his belt.

Lourdis was nearly as big as Crawker; he was thick around the waist, but just not as tall. He had narrow set eyes that never seemed to be still. They were always darting this way and that, never focusing on one thing for more than a few seconds.

The two men noticed him right away when they entered the store. Crawker slapped the back of his hand against Lourdis's chest and motioned at Jeremiah with a toss of his head, alerting his buddy to Jeremiah's presence.

Lourdis grinned and mimicked Jeremiah's limp as he shuffled towards him. "It's the gimp with a limp who looks like a chimp." His eyes twitched, flitting about in their sockets.

Crawker bust out laughing.

Jeremiah bristled, but kept his tongue. So what I got a cleft lip? So what I got a gimp leg? That's how I was delivered into this world. They got no right to scorn me for that.

Crawker moved over to Jeremiah. "Store's all out of bananas, chimp with a limp who's a gimp." Crawker smiled a mighty proud-of-himself smile.

"Find any nuggets out there, gimp?" Lourdis asked.

"Check his butt hole," Crawker said. "He's probably got them stuffed in there."

"Let's see, gimp. Show us what you got hiding in there." Lourdis grabbed Jeremiah's arm and tugged him roughly to him. Jeremiah stumbled and fell to his knees on the wooden floorboards. Lourdis yanked him back upright, crushing Jeremiah against his beefy body. "No need to pray to your betters, gimp."

Henry Crawker hooted.

"Leave him be," Hayman protested, but Jeremiah knew the store owner's words would go unheeded as they always did. Hayman was afraid of the two big men, just as much as he was. He wasn't going to stop them. He never did. The two big men ignored the store owner completely.

Lourdis gripped Jeremiah's arms tight, holding him up for Crawker's approach.

Jeremiah tried to squirm, but Lourdis's grip was savagely strong. He could barely move at all in his painful grasp. His breath whistled in and out.

"Ain't that sweet," Lourdis said. "He's whistlin' me a tune."

Crawker tugged at Jeremiah's pants, pulling them down to his ankles. He took a sharp step back. "Would you look at all the hair on that chimp's ass! That just ain't human."

"Let me see." Lourdis spun Jeremiah around to get a look at his buttocks. "God damn, that's a tangled fucking mess." Lourdis spun him back around.

A tear slipped out of Jeremiah's eye and rolled down his cheek.

"Hey, Crawker. The chimp is crying," Lourdis said.

Crawker nodded. "I seen monkeys cry. Especially when they is scared."

Lourdis frowned at Crawker. "Since when the hell you ever seen a monkey cry before?"

"At the circus in Chicago. I seen it."

Lourdis nodded. He motioned downwards with his head towards Jeremiah's buttocks. "You gonna check him for nuggets or what?"

"Man, I ain't touching that."

"Well, stick a pole in there or something. See what you find." Lourdis shoved Jeremiah away from him.

Jeremiah's feet got caught up in his pants and he crashed to the floor, smacking his chin on the hard wood. The coppery taste of blood filled his mouth, but he just swallowed it.

"You want me to go fishing for gold in his butt hole?" Crawker asked.

Lourdis looked around the store for a quick moment, then grabbed a pickaxe out of a barrel nearby. He held it up to Crawker. Lourdis's spasmodic gaze moved from the axe, to Crawker, to Jeremiah, then back to the axe again.

"That tip looks mighty sharp," Crawker said.

"Don't it, though," Lourdis said. He flipped the pickaxe around in his hand so the thick handle faced away from him. He motioned to Jeremiah with a toss of his head. "Spread him. I have a feeling I'm gonna have to go in deep."

Jeremiah crouched in the stream. He was naked from the waist down, letting the cool water stream past his red and swollen buttocks. One of these days he would pay those two bastards back. In spades. He forced the unpleasant memory of his trip to town aside and moved upstream.

Would the rest of her be here? He thought of the wanted poster he had seen in Hayman's Market. Did the body parts belong to her? His panning tray sat on the nearby rocks, empty of any silt. Unused. He had already found a severed leg, which now rested on the soft grass just beyond the stream's bank.

He knew there was a jumble of rocks just around the bend to the north of his current position. Maybe some of Jezebel was stuck there. He wasn't sure where the name had come from. It had just popped into his head and stuck. Jeremiah and Jezebel. He liked the sound of it.

He moved through the rocks, fishing through the water, probing at anything and everything that he saw. His instincts were right. He found her torso lodged between two boulders. He tugged it out and pulled it back downstream where he joined it with the leg he had found earlier. The body parts fused together, just as the hands had re-joined with the arms. A ghost of a seam was visible where the leg melded back into the torso.

Jeremiah stared at the dark tangle of hair at the bottom of the torso. Jezebel wasn't blonde, but that was okay with him. He liked dark-haired women, too. Her breasts were small, somewhat shriveled by the water. That was okay. He liked small-breasted women, too. He stared at the folds of her womanhood, knowing full well what he was going to do with that later. Don't you think it, Jeremiah. That's just not right. That just ain't right at all. Why not? A man deserves a little pleasure, don't he? Those sons a bitches in town give me nothing but grief. A man's gotta get some relief every once in a while, don't he?

That's when he saw the head floating in the water. He saw it heading towards him down the stream. He just knew it was Jezebel. The eddies took her right towards a rock and he quickly splashed through the stream, his entire body tensing up. He didn't want her to hit no rock. Not his Jezebel. Her head picked up speed and the current pushed her straight towards a jagged rock. Jeremiah splashed wildly through the water, trying to speed up, but the thigh-high water kept him at a slower pace.

Her head hit the rock and Jeremiah saw it cut into her cheek. "No!" he cried. He finally reached her and snatched her out of the water, cradling her head in his arms. She stared up at him with deep hazel eyes. "I'm sorry, Jezebel," he muttered. "I'm so sorry." Jeremiah rocked her head gently back and forth.

Jezebel was nearly whole again. Her arms and legs were reattached to her torso, her nearly complete body resting on the floor next to his table. A blanket was spread out beneath her body. The only thing missing to make her complete was her head. He hadn't gotten up the nerve yet to see if it would reattach itself.

Jeremiah looked down at the head that rested on the nearby table. There was a cruel smirk to her lips, the same cruel smirk he had seen on the sketch hanging in Hayman's Market. She had slightly raised cheekbones and a rounded chin. Her eyes were brown, not blue like he had first imagined. But that was okay. He liked women with brown eyes, too. Every time he glanced at her head, the eyes seemed to be watching him. He felt like they were watching him no matter where he stood in the room.

He poured a touch of alcohol on a towel and wiped at the cut on her cheek. There was no blood to clean, but he just felt like it was the right thing to do. It was his fault for not reaching her in time before the rock cut her.

Jeremiah set that towel down and grabbed a fresh one. He wet the towel in a nearby bowl of water and rubbed some soap onto the fabric. He gently wiped away the dirt and grime from Jezebel's face. He reached her lips and gently wiped around them, cleaning away the dirt. He put a finger to her lips and gently ran it across them. Then he slid his finger inside her mouth. Nothing happened. He moved his finger out of her mouth, and then slid it back in. This time the lips moved. He eased his finger out of her mouth, then eased it back in. The lips started to suck on his finger.

He looked down at his crotch. Don't you do it, Jeremiah. Don't you even think it. That just ain't right.

Jeremiah cradled her head in his arms like a newborn babe. "You ready, Jezebel?" he asked her in a gentle voice.

Her sweet brown eyes just stared up at him.

Jeremiah glanced down. Her headless body still lay prone on the floor on top of the blanket he had set out for her. He moved down to his knees and gently set her head down next to her body, positioning her neck right next to her torso. Her head immediately fused on to her body.

Jeremiah watched her, his breath moving in and out in quick bursts, whistling through his teeth; every muscle in his body was tight.

Her eyes still stared straight up, not blinking. Then her lips moved and she spoke. "Oh, this is nice," she said. Her head slowly turned towards him and she looked straight at Jeremiah. "Hello."

Jeremiah started and fell, falling clumsily back away from her. He quickly righted himself and clambered to his feet.

Then Jezebel sat up. She raised her hands and stared down at them, turning them this way and that, studying them.

Jeremiah could only watch her in amazed silence.

Jezebel rose up off the blanket and stood up. She looked around the cabin for a brief moment before turning her full attention on him.

Jeremiah continued to stare at her in silence.

"You likin' what you see, mister?" Jezebel asked.

She stood naked before him. He could barely see the seams in her skin where her flesh had rejoined. Her breasts weren't wrinkled any more. They were firm and pert and smooth, her nipples pointed and erect. His gaze lingered on her breasts, then moved down to her smooth stomach, and then to the dark patch of curly hair between her legs.

"No need to answer," she said.

Jeremiah looked at her, still trying to fathom what

was happening before his very eyes. "How is this possible?" he finally asked.

She was quiet for a moment. "I still got business here," she said. "That's the only reason I can figure."

Jeremiah looked at her face for a moment, forcing his gaze to move back up to her eyes and away from her womanly hair and her breasts, but he didn't always succeed. "What kind of business?" he finally asked.

The cruel smirk on her lips grew more pronounced. "Lots of people done me wrong. And lots of people are gonna pay."

"They said you..." Jeremiah hesitated, licking at his cleft.

Jezebel stood silently, waiting for him to continue.

"They said you butchered half a dozen men and stole their gold."

Jezebel frowned. "Is that what they say?" She raised up her hand and pointed at her chest. "Well, *I* say I found a fat vein and two dozen men gang raped me and stole my gold. *I* say I killed half a dozen men to get *my* gold back. That's what I say."

Jeremiah watched her for a long moment, his gaze once again roaming all over naked body. He looked back up at her face. She never blinked. Her gaze just riveted him to the spot he was standing in. All he could do was stare with absolute fascination at the resurrected woman before him. "You were dead." It was an obvious statement and he felt foolish for saying it aloud after it left his lips.

She nodded. "Yes, I was. And then you brought me back. Why did you do that?"

Jeremiah didn't answer her question. Her erect nipples kept pulling his gaze to them like fire light on a dark night. "How?" he muttered. "How is this even possible?" he asked again.

Jezebel smiled and shook her head. "Must be there ain't no room for me in Heaven no more, not after what I've done. And maybe cause I ain't gonna let no one drag me to Hell." She shook her head more insistently. "No, sir. Not yet. I'm staying here as long as I can." She looked at him. "Besides, I told you. I still got work to do here."

"Don't you think you should — just move on?" he finally wondered aloud.

She smiled. "And miss all the fun still to be had on this side of Hell?" She shook her head.

"Maybe you is just scared of passing on," he said. "Scared of leaving this world."

"I look scared to you?" she asked.

He didn't answer.

Jezebel looked intently at him. "You got some scared in you, mister. I can see it in those soft little eyes you got. But that ain't foolin' me. You got some hate in there, too, don't ya? Some hate just as dark as mine." She looked at him and smiled her dark smile. "Maybe that's what brought me back."

Jeremiah said nothing. His gaze again roamed over her naked body.

"That's enough of that talk," Jezebel said. "I'm trying to have a serious conversation with you and you keep looking at my tits and my pussy." She moved over to the bed and laid down on the mattress on her back. She looked over at Jeremiah.

Jeremiah just stared.

"Well, don't just stand there, mister." She slowly spread her legs, revealing the soft folds of her womanhood. "Come and get your reward." She reached down between her legs and spread herself for him.

"You want me... to come over there?"

Jezebel patted the mattress. "Sure I do, mister. Ain't that what you brought me back for?"

"My name is Jeremiah."

"Okay, Jeremiah. Come on over here." She waved her hand at him, again motioning for him to join her on the bed.

"Your name is Jezebel," he stated.

She looked at him with a slight tilt of her head. "I know my own name, Jeremiah. Now are you coming over here?" She cupped her breasts and squeezed them firmly. Her erect nipples pointed at him from between her fingers.

He moved awkwardly to the side of the bed.

"Don't be shy now. You already put your dick in my mouth, remember?"

Jeremiah felt his cheeks blazing hot and red. "That makes me just as bad as them, don't it? Just as bad as them men you killed."

She reached up and took his hand, tugging him down onto the bed. She shook her head softly. "I was the one sucked your finger first."

He looked at her, then looked away, lowering his head. "I ain't never kissed no woman before."

"Why not?"

He pointed to his cleft lip. "They don't take a shine to that."

Jezebel raised her head up and kissed him full and firm on his lips. She pulled back and gave his cleft a soft lick. "Well, I like it. Gives you character."

Her hands were warm on his skin as she undressed him. She wasn't cold and clammy when he lay on top of her. She was warm and willing. Jeremiah slid inside of her and Jezebel was warm in there, too. Somehow, she was very warm and very wet. He didn't know what was going to happen next, but for now it was all worth it. He moved deeper into her and clutched at her, kissing her hard on her willing mouth. Hayman was wrong. She was a lady of love after all.

Jeremiah sat on the edge of the bed. He had fornicated with Jezebel three times, twice releasing into her in the missionary position and once when he took her from behind because she asked him to fuck her that way. He was satiated and exhausted. And nervous. Very nervous. He glanced over at his axe resting against a nearby wall. "You gonna kill me now?" His breath came out in shrill whistles.

Jezebel smiled. "Jeremiah, I'm never gonna kill you." She reached up and caressed his cheek. "Not after what you done for me." She let her smile slip just a bit. "Let me restate that. If I find you with another woman, I *will* kill you, and then I'll kill her. We clear on that? I don't take kindly to anyone stealin' my gold or my man."

Jeremiah nodded. "Yes, ma'am." He felt the tension ease from his shoulders and a grin crossed his lips.

Jezebel gave him a sweet kiss on his lips. "Good." She rose up off the bed and grabbed the axe from its spot against the wall. "Let's go prospecting for a little bit o' vengeance." She raised the axe up and twirled the heavy chopping tool in her hand. "Now who's pissing you off the most?"

Hayman worked at a long table in the back room of his store, chiseling the name Samuel Lourdis into the second of two freshly cut tombstones. The first tombstone was finished, the name Henry Crawker already etched into the rock.

Just outside the room, two posters hung on a wall. One was a sketch of a woman with a pretty face and a cruel smirk. Her poster was crinkled and marred with dozens of folds. The **$500** next to the big bold word **REWARD** was crossed off with a big black X and a **$1000** was scribbled in above the scratched out number.

The second wanted poster was freshly printed, the sketch of a man with a pug nose and a cleft lip filling the top half of the paper. A **$1000 REWARD** was offered for his capture. Dead or alive.

"A very short time will serve to calm down the fever of excitement that at present exists; and in California, as everywhere else, the hardworking, steady and honest will succeed and become rich and prosperous... and if to attain these benefits there is at first a little difficulty, and even some suffering and misery, it must be remembered that no important good can be had without such drawbacks, and that the advantage will be permanent, while the evil is very temporary."

- From The Gold-Seekers Manual by David T. Ansted, M.A. F.R.S.

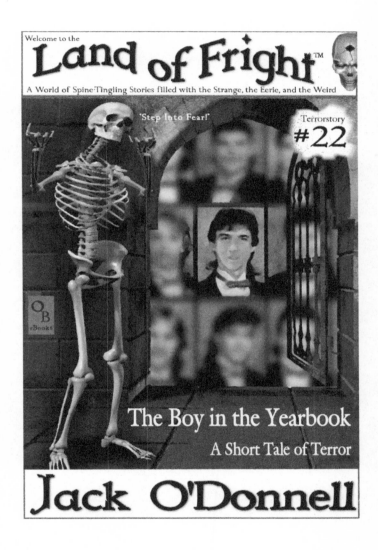

Welcome to the

Land of Fright™

A World of Spine-Tingling Stories filled with the Strange, the Eerie, and the Weird

"Step Into Fear!"

Terrorstory
#22

The Boy in the Yearbook

A Short Tale of Terror

Jack O'Donnell

TERRORSTORY #22
THE BOY IN THE YEARBOOK

"**I**t was him. I'm telling you, it was him," Joslyn York said, the nervous fear in her voice impossible to miss. She was a slender woman with a head of tight brunette curls and brown eyes. She stood in her friend's laundry room in her basement. A muted beam of sunlight filtered in from the window well above the dryer.

"Who?"

"Him, Terry. Him."

Terry McCarthy froze. For a moment, Joslyn's friend couldn't speak. "Are you sure?" Terry asked. Terry had put on some weight since their high school glory days and her plump cheeks were ruddy with excited nervousness. Her black hair had a hint of grey starting to creep its way to the surface. Terry had been dyeing it for a while, but had given up doing that years ago; too much money and too much effort.

"I'm sure," Joslyn said. "I know his face. He looks almost exactly the same."

Terry stood motionless for a long moment, then set her son's grass-stained soccer shirt down on top of the washing machine.

Him. Joslyn knew Terry understood exactly who she was talking about. He was the one common bond from their past that would never be broken. Or at least not until the mystery of who he was got solved. It had been a different time back when they were in high school together. There had been no internet. No ubiquitous camera phones. No selfies. Seeing yourself in a group picture was actually exciting and special. She remembered how she and Terry had been so eager to get their hands on their high school yearbook. There were several different photos of themselves scattered throughout the yearbook. One of them was an action photo of them playing soccer. God, they were so hot back then. So young and vigorous, so full of energy and enthusiasm. Another photo was of them in Art club, their faces and arms smeared with a rainbow of paint colors, their smiles big and bright. A third yearbook photograph was of them sitting and laughing in the cafeteria. Joslyn remembered the first time they found their portraits amidst all the other students in their grade and they tittered and teased each other over their photos. They drooled over Billy Cole and Gino and Zach and a dozen other studs.

And then there was that one picture. The one picture neither of them could get out of their heads. Even now after more than twenty years had passed.

A picture of him. The boy she and Terry could not remember even though they had known everyone in their class. There were only sixty five kids in their graduating class, so they either knew everyone or were at least familiar with who everyone was. But not him. He had a dark look to him, with dark European features and a strong nose. But it was his eyes that captivated them. His eyes were what grabbed hold of them every time they looked at his yearbook portrait. Eyes that looked like they held an infinite pool of something. Of what, she wasn't sure. Sadness. Rage. Contempt. Hopelessness. Every time Joslyn looked at his eyes in the yearbook photograph she saw something different in them. Had he been a last minute transfer student? Some kid who had just moved in? No, she knew he hadn't been. Something deep inside her told her that wasn't true. He had always been a student at the school. He wasn't some new kid. So who was he? And why couldn't they remember him?

"Where did you see him?" Terry asked. She rubbed a stain stick across the grass stains and dropped the shirt into the washing machine. She reached down to grab another shirt from the clothes basket at her feet.

"At the school," Joslyn said. "I went to pick up

Denise. And there he was. Standing in the hallway."

"You saw him at the school? Jesus…" Terry was quiet for a moment. She looked down at the muddy shirt in her hand, then back up at Joslyn. "Are you sure? Maybe you were just —"

"I wasn't *just* anything. I wasn't imagining him. I wasn't seeing things. It was him, Terry. I swear on my kids' souls it was him."

"Don't do that," Terry said.

"Do what?"

"Swear on your kids' souls. Don't do that."

Joslyn brushed off her comment with a dismissive wave of her hand.

Terry was quiet. "Did he… say anything? Do anything?"

Joslyn shook her head. "No, he just stood in the hallway. Fucking watching me." She shivered. "I need a shower just from the look he gave me."

"Was he… our age?"

Joslyn frowned at her. "What?"

"Was he our age? Was he older?"

"Of course he was older." Joslyn looked at Terry. "What, you think maybe he's a ghost? You think I'm fucking seeing ghosts?"

Terry shrugged. "Maybe. Maybe he was some kid trapped here. You know, some lost spirit who can't pass over." Terry looked at Joslyn. "But you said he was older. For sure? For sure he was older?"

Joslyn nodded. "For sure. He looked late-thirties. Maybe forties. Same face. Just older."

"Ghosts don't grow older." Terry's voice was soft, barely audible.

"What?"

"Nothing. I just don't think he's a ghost. Ghosts

don't grow older."

"How do you know that?" Joslyn asked.

Terry closed the lid of the washing machine, but made no move to start the machine. "What? You think ghosts age like us?"

Joslyn shrugged. "Who the fuck knows?"

"So you think he could be a ghost, too?"

"I don't know what the hell he is. I just know he's freaking me out." Joslyn fidgeted from one foot to the other. "What if he's after Denise? What if he's some kind of sick pedophile?"

"Jesus."

"I have to go see Barbara," Joslyn said. "This is creeping me out way too much. I feel like I'm about to lose it."

"Would you like to lie on the couch?" Barbara Galligan-Creel asked Joslyn. Barbara was in her mid-sixties, aging gracefully with a few soft wrinkles around her eyes and the corners of her mouth. She had dark hair and dark features. She was dressed professionally in a dark blue pantsuit. A tablet rested in her lap. They were in Barbara's psychiatric office. The furniture was lush mahogany, polished to a sharp gleam. A few potted plants dotted the far wall. The curtains were drawn, keeping the harsh sunlight at bay. A soft floor lamp illuminated the room in a gentle glow.

"No, I'd actually like to tell the truth on the couch," Joslyn said.

Barbara smiled. "You always were the witty one.

Vulgar, but witty."

Joslyn frowned. She moved over to the couch and sat down. "You're supposed to be helping me, doc. Not insulting me."

Barbara looked at her. "Are you saying you are not witty? Or not vulgar?"

Joslyn waved her hand. "Okay, fuck, I am the witty one."

"What brings you in to see me, Joslyn?"

Joslyn was quiet for a moment. "I saw him today."

Barbara was quiet.

"You know who I'm talking about, don't you?"

"I believe I do, yes." Barbara moved her stylus, making a note on the tablet.

Joslyn remained sitting upright. "I saw him in the school. In the hallway."

Barbara waited for her to continue.

"He was just standing there." Joslyn laid down on the couch and put her arm over her forehead. "Why am I suddenly seeing him again? Everything was going so well. Skip and I are even fucking again."

"I think you know why."

"Yeah, because I'm happy. I'm sabotaging my own happiness." Joslyn paused. "How fucked up is that?"

"Deep seated guilt can do that to anyone."

"Deep seated guilt?" Joslyn was quiet for a moment. "I might do some things here and there that might not be right. Sure, I download some music and some movies I really should pay for, but they're always charging too much for that shit anyway. I only sneak a smoke when no one else is around and I always smoke outside." She paused for a moment. "I mean, I can look at other men, right? As long as I don't touch. I don't think my guilt could be called deep seated."

"Flirting can be harmful. To both parties involved."

Joslyn flicked her wrist. "Nah, flirting is harmless fun."

"Is it? It wasn't harmless for Joey Galligan."

Joslyn frowned and looked over at Barbara. "Who's Joey Galligan?"

Barbara looked at her for a moment, then leaned in closer. "Joey Galligan was my son," she whispered.

And then Joslyn remembered. She remembered who the boy in the yearbook was. And she remembered what they had done to him.

They had killed him. Oh, they hadn't meant to, but it happened all the same. Joey had been so naive, and so trusting. It was easy to tease him and trick him into doing stuff.

She and Terry teased him with a threesome. They paraded around him in their super tight shorts and their tight T's. The day they both went bra-less to school was a big day. Her nipples got so hard. Joslyn distinctly remembered that. It was wildly, weirdly erotic knowing that Joey saw them through the nearly sheer fabric she had been wearing. She and Terry were both called down to the principal's office and were scolded by old man Johnstone and got sent home, but it had been worth it. The look on Joey's face had been worth it. They knew he wanted them. They knew he wanted them both.

Joey was a nice looking boy. Joslyn remembered

how she and Terry watched him in gym class. He was a little bit awkward, and not the greatest athlete, but he was damn cute in his tight gym shorts. She remembered the first time they had played dodge ball and he had purposely missed her so she could stay in the game. Joey had her dead in his sights, but he held up his throw and let her scramble away before throwing the ball at the spot she had just vacated. It was a simple gesture, but it had endeared him to her immediately.

One night, they invited him over to do homework. He was good at math and they both sucked at it, so there was at least some truth to them telling Joey that they needed his help with some of the equation problems. What he didn't know was that Joslyn's parents were gone for the weekend and they would have the house to themselves. That was pretty exciting stuff for eighteen-year-olds. She had just turned eighteen three weeks earlier. Terry had already been eighteen for months. "Hey, we're adults now," they told Joey. They kissed each other in front of Joey and laughed. They hugged each other, blatantly rubbing their breasts together. The look on Joey's face was priceless.

What Joey didn't know either was that Joslyn knew where the key to the liquor cabinet was. They started off with a shot of whiskey. They all gagged and sputtered at the harsh bite of the liquor. But then the warmth in their belly and the tingling buzz in their brains made the next shot go down a little smoother. They chased the third shot with some cola and that made it even better.

They decided to go to the park. It was only half a block away from Joslyn's house. They walked there, laughing and giggling. The night was warm and pleasant. The streets were empty and quiet, illuminated with the soft glow of the streetlights. Joslyn remembered Terry grabbing Joey's arm and rubbing her tits all over him as she pretended to stumble over a curb. Joslyn remembered she grabbed his ass, squeezed it, and ran away from him laughing. Joey chased them both into the park.

Thick wooden logs marked off the equipment area where the swings and the slides were. The concrete surface of the playground area wasn't covered with wood chips or that chopped-up black rubber like all playgrounds were now. It was just hard stone. There was also a monkey bar set up in the classic metal geodesic shape. And there was the merry-go-round. The flat circular metal platform with the eight spindly metal arms that you clutched onto while it spun round and round. That's where Joey died.

"Hey, look what I brought," Terry said, swinging the whiskey bottle back and forth.

"You can't have booze in the park. That's illegal," Joey said. He was always such a straight laced kid, Joslyn remembered. At least until that night.

Terry waved the bottle again. "Silly boy." Terry took a swig straight from the bottle. It was too much for her and she had to spit it out. "Uggh, that tastes worse than Zach did."

Joslyn laughed and ripped the bottle out of Terry's hand. She handed it to Joey. "Here. Your turn. Terry can't hold her liquor." Joslyn paused for comedic effect. "Cause I swiped it from her, ha ha."

Joey shook his head. Joslyn distinctly remembered that. He hadn't wanted any more. She should have stopped teasing him right there. She should have stopped goading him on. They should've gone home. But she didn't stop. "No, I'm good," he said.

Joslyn shook her head. "No. I'm good." She put the neck of the bottle to her mouth and sucked on it. She glanced up to see if Joey was watching her. He was. She slowly pulled the neck of the bottle out of her mouth and tilted it towards Joey.

Terry stumbled up behind Joslyn and hugged her, cupping her breasts in her hands. "Come on, Joey. Don't you want some of this?"

Joey didn't say anything. He just stared.

"If you drink, you get us both," Joslyn told him.

Terry nodded and smiled playfully at him. She slid her hand down to Joslyn's crotch and rubbed it. Joslyn held the bottle out to Joey. He took it. And he drank.

They made him do all sorts of stuff, teasing him, egging him on. Go down the slide backwards, Joey. Hang upside down on the monkey bars, Joey. Joslyn let him put his hand down her pants after that one, and let him feel how wet she was over the fabric of her panties.

They kept drinking. He kept drinking.

They made Joey pull his pants down to show it to them. It was nice. Nothing spectacular, but his cock was nice. They made him get on the merry-go-round with his pants around his ankles. They spun him faster and faster and faster. They laughed hysterically. He had to really hold on tight to keep himself from falling over. "Jump," Joslyn told him. "Jump off," Terry said. They spun Joey faster and faster, laughing crazily as the metal platform picked up speed. They both kept chanting, "Jump. Jump. Jump."

And he did. Joslyn and Terry whooped with crazy

laughter as Joey flung himself off the madly spinning merry-go-round.

And then Joey died. He hit the ground at a weird angle and Joslyn remembered hearing something snapping as his body contorted into an unnatural position. At first they thought he was just fooling them when he didn't move. But when he didn't move at all for a few minutes, they went over to him. They both stared down at him. Blood pooled out of Joey's mouth and dripped over his chin. His neck was crooked, hanging at an angle that just didn't seem possible. It was disgusting. His eyes were open and glassy.

Joslyn and Terry just ran, leaving Joey Galligan dead and alone in the playground with his pants around his ankles.

Barbara watched Joslyn's body shake uncontrollably. She leaned back in her chair. Barbara's eyes were dark and cold, but a satisfied smile still came to her lips. The fresh pain on the woman's face, the shock of the guilt overwhelming Joslyn, was immensely satisfying to witness. Barbara never grew tired of it.

"It's okay, Joslyn," Barbara said. "Let it all come out. Let all that guilt come pouring out." *And then we'll put it all back in.*

"How could I have forgotten that?" Tears streamed down Joslyn's face as she shakily moved to a sitting position on the couch, the wet trails of sorrow muddying her makeup. "We —" The words didn't come out as more sobs choked her throat. She fought back the convulsive gasps, forcing herself to be calm. "We killed him."

"Yes, you did," Barbara said. "That's why you come to see me. So I can help you forget." *And then help you remember it all over again.*

Joslyn swiped at her tears. "You make me forget?"

Barbara nodded. "Yes. Through hypnosis. I've been helping you block it. The mental block the hypnosis puts in place doesn't last forever, so that's why we need to continue our sessions." *Forever.*

Joslyn frowned. "I don't remember doing any hypnosis with you before."

Barbara smiled. "Exactly. That's the point. That's how effective it is."

Joslyn rubbed at her temples. "How long have we been doing this hypnosis thing, doc?"

"About twenty years."

"Twenty years?" Joslyn shook her head. "Twenty years," she repeated. "Twenty years. How is that possible? I've been living with this for twenty years..." Her voice trailed off as she continued to struggle with the ramifications of what had just been revealed to her.

"A long time," Barbara said, acknowledging the duration.

"Shouldn't I be better by now?" Joslyn asked.

"Oh, you are better," Barbara said with a smile. "You should have seen yourself when you first started."

"I don't remember..." Suddenly, more tears streamed down out of Joslyn's eyes, further smearing the makeup on her face. "I don't remember. What's happening to me?" She buried her face in her hands and sobbed.

Barbara watched her quietly.

Joslyn looked up, her cheeks wet with grief. "How can I live with myself? We killed that boy."

"Joey. His name was Joey."

Joslyn paused for a moment, then nodded slightly, the tears still coming. She wiped at some of the wetness on her face with the back of her hand. "Joey. We killed Joey."

Barbara nodded. "That's why you are here. So I can help you." *So I can help you re-live it. Over and over again.*

Joslyn was quiet for a long moment. "It was an accident." Her words came out with a questioning lilt to them. "That poor boy. I can't believe we did that." She looked up at Barbara after a long moment of staring blankly at the carpeting at her feet. "Did that really happen?"

Barbara nodded. "Yes, it did."

"I feel so fuzzy right now. I feel really disoriented."

Barbara gently touched her shoulder. "You need to lay back down. I can start the hypnosis now. It will help you forget."

Joslyn remained sitting upright. "Maybe I shouldn't forget. Maybe I should remember."

"Is that how you want to live the rest of your life?"

"It will fade, won't it? I mean time heals all wounds, right?" She wiped at her cheeks again. "Maybe I should just deal with it. It was a long time ago."

"We can't let that happen," Barbara said. *I won't let that happen.*

Joslyn looked at her curiously.

"Do you want to go to jail?" Barbara asked. "Think about your children."

Joslyn frowned.

"We need to repress those memories so you don't accidentally say something or do something that could incriminate you," Barbara said.

"Isn't there some kind of statute of limitations?"

"Not for murder."

"Murder?" A flash of fear flared up in Joslyn's eyes. She shook her head, the motion vigorous and sharp. "No, it was an accident."

Barbara said nothing.

"Aren't you supposed to report me or something? Tell the police?"

And deprive myself of this? Barbara shook her head. "No. I'm your psychiatrist. What happens in this room stays in this room."

"Just like in Vegas, right?" Joslyn tried to laugh, but only managed an awkward splutter.

Barbara did not laugh.

Joslyn was quiet. "It was an accident," she said again.

Barbara's expression remained even. "Let's begin the hypnosis. You are obviously distraught."

Joslyn frowned. "I don't know, doc. I don't think I want to be hypnotized."

"Just think of it as mental make-up that temporarily covers up your blemishes. Whenever you start to think of Joey again, that means the effects of the hypnotism are wearing off. That's why you start to see him again. And when you see him you get nervous and agitated. That's what these sessions are for. That's why you are here today, isn't it? To stop feeling so nervous and agitated," Barbara said.

Joslyn nodded docilely.

"We just need to re-apply the hypnotism when its power starts to fade." Barbara motioned at the couch. "Now go ahead and lay down."

"I — okay." Joslyn nodded wearily and moved back to a prone position on the couch.

Barbara tapped her tablet. A soft, steady monotone sound started playing. "Just concentrate on the sound," Barbara said, her voice calm and soothing. "This is the hypnotic induction phase that lets your mind rest and prepare it for treatment. Go ahead, close your eyes and listen to the sound."

Joslyn hesitated for a moment, then closed her eyes.

"Concentrate on the sound." Barbara could see Joslyn starting to relax. The tightness in the woman's features started to lessen. "Now press your thumb and forefinger together."

Joslyn did as she was asked.

"Hold your breath for a count of five, then release both your breath and fingers while letting your mind drift." Barbara kept her voice soft, soothing. "Good. Repeat that again. Press your thumb and forefinger together. Hold your breath. Good. Listen to the sound. Now breathe out slowly and let your fingers relax. Good." This went on for a few minutes until Barbara was certain Joslyn was relaxed. "Go ahead and open your eyes."

Joslyn opened her eyes and Barbara could see from the glassy look in her eyes that Joslyn was receptive, her mental state ready for the next step. "I created some phrases that help hypnotize you," Barbara said. "I'm going to lean in and whisper one of them to you." She glanced over to her desk at the photograph of a young boy in the frame. He had a dark look to him, with dark European features and a strong nose. She turned back towards Joslyn and leaned in closer. "Joey Galligan will grow old with you and haunt you forever."

The look on Joslyn's face changed immediately. She lay very still on the couch, her eyes staring but looking at nothing, seeing nothing. She appeared lost for a long moment, unsure of her surroundings. Finally, after a few more moments had passed, she blinked.

Barbara tapped her tablet, turning off the monotone sound.

Joslyn's gaze found Barbara and she smiled. "Hey, doc. Sorry, I must have dozed off." She reached up and touched her wet cheeks. "Was I crying in my sleep again?"

Barbara looked at her. "It's good. Your body is just releasing toxins." She smiled warmly. She knew Joslyn had no memory of what had just transpired in her office. The hypnotic phrase wiped away the memories of their initial talk about Joey. For all Joslyn knew, she had just woken up from a quick unexpected nap in her office before their session had even started. "Feel better? You were pretty tired when you first got here. That's why I had you lay down for a minute." She smiled at Joslyn. "You were out like a light."

"Yeah." Joslyn looked up at Barbara from her prone position on the couch. "Yeah, I do feel better. I still feel tired, but better."

Barbara nodded. "You ready to start?"

Joslyn nodded. "Sure."

They had a delightful session, talking about

Joslyn's husband, her children, her job, her life, her dreams. They talked a lot about her daughter Denise, about how well she was doing in school, about how proud Joslyn was of her good grades. They finished with warm smiles and cheerful words.

"I'll see you next month," Barbara said and set her tablet down on her desk next to the picture of her son.

Joslyn looked at the photo of the boy in the picture frame on Barbara's desk. "Who's that?" she asked.

"That's my son," Barbara said. "That's his high school picture."

"He's cute," Joslyn said. She stared at the picture of the boy for a long moment, studying it with a curious expression. "I feel like I know him."

Barbara smiled. "You ought to pull out your high school yearbook. Sometimes reminiscing about the dreams you had for your life in the past can help you plan goals for the future."

Joslyn was quiet for a moment, thinking. "You know what? I think I might just do that when I get home."

Barbara nodded gently. She had planted the suggestion in Joslyn years ago that every time she told her to look at her high school yearbook Joslyn would do just that. Joslyn would see the picture of Joey's portrait and that would trigger him to slowly start appearing to her. And that would drive Joslyn right back to her for another session.

"Thanks, doc." Joslyn slowly rose up to her feet. She staggered for a moment, but quickly retained her balance. "Wow, these sessions really take a lot out of me."

"Unburdening your soul is hard work." Barbara smiled gaily at Joslyn. "Tell Terry I look forward to seeing her next week."

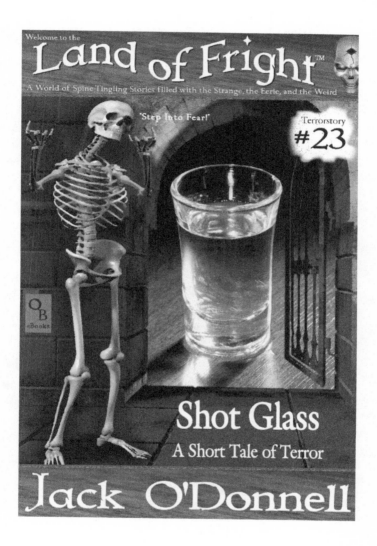

Welcome to the
Land of Fright™
A World of Spine-Tingling Stories filled with the Strange, the Eerie, and the Weird

"Step Into Fear!"

Terrorstory
#23

Shot Glass
A Short Tale of Terror

Jack O'Donnell

TERRORSTORY #23
SHOT GLASS

"**T**oo bad about that promotion. Better luck next time."

"Yeah, rub it in, you piece of shit. You know I deserved that more than you did." Jeff Grandlin paused. "I guess I've been sucking the wrong cock." Jeff was in his early thirties, with short brown hair. A few old acne scars dotted his face with tiny craters. He was dressed in faded jeans and a pretty severely wrinkled pale blue collared shirt.

"Yeah, you should be sucking mine right about now," Wasim Lanjwani said. Wasim was in his late twenties, with a dark Pakistani complexion and black hair. He was dressed in black dress pants and a freshly ironed white collared shirt. The Fallon Manufacturing logo was sewn into the left breast of the shirt.

"From what I hear that toothpick would give me splinters," Jeff said.

The two men were standing near the food table at their annual corporate shin ding. The table was full of tiny sandwiches, pieces of cheese and fruit cut into the shapes of some of the parts they fabricated, and pastries with their corporate logo drawn in icing on the tops. Around them, dozens of fellow employees from the Fallon Manufacturing company milled about, talking, drinking, laughing. They had a pretty decent quarter so bonus checks were definitely a possibility this year.

"Who'd you hear that from?" Wasim asked around a mouthful of the finger sandwich he was eating.

"Why, from your dear old mother." Jeff paused. "After she spit out my load, of course. At least she has the decency to know that she shouldn't talk with her mouth full." He grabbed a chunk of cheese from a nearby plate and popped it into his mouth.

Wasim just stared at him for a quiet moment. "And you wonder why you got passed up?" He finished off the rest of his sandwich and licked his fingers.

Jeff finished chewing the cheese and swallowed. "Yeah," he said. He paused for a moment and then gave Wasim a playful shove on his shoulder. "Hey, I'm just being a bitter dick. Let's celebrate your promotion. Do a shot with me."

Wasim raised his bottle. "I'm doing wine coolers tonight."

"Wine coolers? On the day of your promotion? Come on, man. Live it up a little. One shot of whiskey, that's it. You can chase it with that fruity water. Come on."

"All right." Wasim raised a finger. "But just one."

"Yeah, yeah. Just one."

❦

The day Jeff found his great grandfather's shot glass collection was the greatest day in his life. The shot glasses were hidden in his attic, locked away in a big wooden chest. There were dozens and dozens of them, all of them neatly wrapped in newspaper. He unwrapped a few of the shot glasses and read the inscriptions that were etched or painted onto their sides. Some of them were from US cities like Chicago, Los Angeles, and New York City, while some shot glasses were from faraway exotic lands, with elaborate etchings of foreign city names scratched into or painted on the surface of the glass. Jeff had heard of most of the places, but he had never visited any of them. And as far as he knew, his great grandfather hadn't been much of a traveler either. Where did he get all these? Jeff wondered. He grunted. Most likely from garage sales. That's probably where his mom picked up her junk collecting habit from.

His great grandfather was a cankerous old bastard from Ireland who lived to be nearly a hundred and five. Jeff frowned at the memory of the old man. His mom used to torment him when he was bad and tell him that she was going to send him away to spend a day at Great Grandpa Kyle's house. The threat of that was enough to scare Jeff straight for a few days. Great Grandpa Kyle was just downright creepy, with his long white nose hairs dangling out of his nostrils like

47

branches of a weeping willow tree. His bushy eyebrows reminded Jeff of the hairy caterpillars he used to find in their backyard; he used to stare at those eyebrows, afraid they might start moving and jump off Great Grandpa Kyle's face and attach themselves to his face. And the stark memory of his bad teeth still made Jeff feel nauseous. Jeff had never seen teeth so brown in his life. The fact that the old man was rumored to be a practicing druid from the Irish old country made a visit to Great Grandpa Kyle's house all the more unnerving. Whenever they visited him, the old man would never look straight at any of them; he would just follow them out of the corners of his bloodshot eyes. Freaky.

Jeff unwrapped a few more of the shot glasses and again wondered where they had all come from. He didn't remember moving them into his attic, but then again he didn't remember where half the stuff in his attic had come from. When Great Grandpa Kyle died, Jeff did remember his mother asking him to store some of the old man's stuff until she could figure out what to do with it. But his mother had died before that happened, so Jeff had just left it all in the attic, untouched until now.

At first, Jeff was just going to throw them all away. What the hell use did he have for dozens of stupid shot glasses? But then he discovered the power they held, and he knew he would never part with them.

"Whiskey. Two shots." Jeff handed the bartender a shot glass. "Put one of them in there."

The barkeeper took the shot glass and looked at it.

The words etched on the glass read *Buenos Aires.* "Hey, I've been there," he said. The barkeeper smiled. "Lots of nice muchachas there."

"Yeah. I've got a friend who's about to go there. I think he's gonna love it."

Jeff took the two shots and headed back towards Wasim.

❈⟡❈

Jeff found a beautiful display cabinet behind a dusty old tarp near where he found the shot glasses in the attic. The wood of the shelves reminded Jeff of the yew pipe Great Grandpa Kyle used to smoke. The shelves had the same orange-brown color with the grains in the wood close to each other. Jeff shook his head at the memory of his scary old great grandfather. Great Grandpa Kyle had called it his magic pipe. Jeff remembered the old man waving the pipe at him, telling him it was carved from yew wood from Ireland. The wood was magical, he said. It would last much longer than he ever would.

Jeff studied the cabinet. The display unit was five rows high, with ten slots to a shelf. He cleaned off the shelves, wiping away the decades of dust, then set the shot glasses into the slots. He was amazed that not one of the shot glasses seemed to be missing. Jeff took a step back and studied the display unit. All fifty slots were filled with shot glasses, each one designating a unique location.

He had a sudden irresistible urge to do a shot. Jeff darted downstairs to his liquor stash. He had some vodka, an unopened bottle of gin, and a bottle of half-finished whiskey. He grabbed the whiskey. It seemed the appropriate choice considering his great grandfather's predilection for the stuff. He didn't remember much more about the old man, but that was one of the other things Jeff did remember about his great grandfather. The smell of whiskey on his breath. It was always on his breath. Great Grandpa Kyle had worn that smell like it was an overcoat he could never take off.

It turned out Jeff's choice of liquor had been the right one because it only worked with whiskey. Jeff had no idea why. That's just the way it was. It had to be a shot of whiskey. He had tried the vodka, and had even opened up the gin to give that a try, but neither one of them worked.

Somehow whiskey was the secret. Somehow whiskey unlocked the power stored up in the shot glasses.

Somehow whiskey fueled the teleportation.

Jeff handed Wasim the Buenos Aires shot glass. "Drink it fast in one gulp."

Wasim took the offered shot glass, barely even glancing at it. "I know how to do a shot, shit." He raised the glass and quickly tilted his wrist, downing the whiskey. He scrunched his face into one big pucker. He coughed. "Wow, that is some strong stuff."

Jeff reached out and took the shot glass from Wasim's hand. "You have no idea."

And then, after a moment of Jeff looking curiously at his co-worker, Wasim vanished. Just like that, he was gone. Jeff glanced at the Buenos Aires shot glass and grinned. Enjoy your visit to Argentina, motherfucker. How's that big meeting going to go tomorrow when you're not there? Guess I'll have to fill in for you. Jeff raised his shot glass and downed the whiskey in one gulp.

The first time Jeff teleported nearly sent him straight to the loony bin. He had sucked down a shot of whiskey from one of his great grandfather's shot glasses and seconds later found himself outside, standing on a sidewalk near a busy street. Jeff had no memory of how he got there. He remembered standing on the sidewalk, completely freaked out. What the hell? His mind raced and he could feel a swell of total panic rise up inside his brain. He forced himself to be calm, reciting his name and social security number over and over in his head. It was one technique he used to fight back his panic attacks.

At first, Jeff had no idea where he was, but then familiar storefronts registered in his mind and he recognized where he was. He was on Michigan Avenue, just a few blocks away from Water Tower Place, the tall building brightly lit up for the night. A few shoppers, their arms heavy with bags, brushed right by him. Jeff stood stock still for a long moment, struggling to process what the hell had just happened to him.

Am I in a dream? It didn't feel like a dream. It felt very real. The air around him was cold and biting. Jeff glanced down at the shot glass in his hand. He read the word painted on the side of the glass. *Chicago.* Did I have some kind of weird blackout? That had happened only once in his life, at a wild 4th of July party at his house when he was in high school. He woke up the next morning in his backyard, with one shoe on and the other one nowhere to be found. Firecracker debris littered the ground all around him. A few burn marks singed his clothes. He didn't remember anything about the party at all. Not making out with Lisa Lawrence, not puking all over Reggie. Nothing. Later, his friends told him they were throwing firecrackers at him and he didn't move at all.

Jeff raised the shot glass up to his face and sniffed it. It smelled like normal whiskey. He didn't feel that drunk, or hungover. As the threatening flood of panic receded, he became conscious of the fact that physically he felt good. His body tingled with a slight, pleasant buzz.

Jeff stared at the shot glass in his hand. He had drunk a shot from the Chicago shot glass, and then he was suddenly in Chicago. That was fucked up. How the hell was that possible? He had no idea, but all he could do was try to absorb the actuality of what had happened to him.

Thank God his house was in Evanston, so it wasn't hard to get back home.

The second time Jeff teleported, it wasn't so disorienting, and the slight tingling in his arms and legs right before he teleported wasn't so uncomfortable. He used the same Chicago shot glass. And this time he put on a winter coat before he took the shot. It had been freezing outside the first time he teleported. It had been a damn cold ride home on the

CTA train after his first unexpected trip.

The third time Jeff teleported, he just laughed and went shopping on Michigan Avenue. Got himself a few nice new shirts.

Jeff thought about telling his girlfriend about the shot glasses, but he decided to keep the secret to himself for now. Nancy didn't need to know. Not yet.

Jeff stared at the Hawaii shot glass. Man, that would be great to go to Hawaii. But how the hell do I get home? He stared at the shot glasses that lined the display case in the attic and realized he had his answer staring right back at him. He put the Hawaii shot glass back into its slot on the shelf and grabbed the shot glass that read *Home Sweet Home*. He rolled the cool glass between his fingers. It was obvious.

He put the Home Sweet Home shot glass in his pocket and poured himself two fingers of whiskey into the Chicago shot glass. He downed the whiskey in one quick gulp. The familiar tingling sensation started in his stomach, then radiated up to his chest, and then down to his thighs. The prickling shivers moved up to his shoulders and down to his calves. The tingling moved along his arms and through his feet. Jeff knew he was getting close to launch. The moment the tingling sensation hit the tips of his fingers and the tips off his toes, he would launch. He didn't remember anything about the actual teleportation itself. It was as if he just blinked and then he was suddenly somewhere else.

He always teleported to the same spot on Michigan Avenue when he used the Chicago shot glass. He didn't feel like shopping or sightseeing on this trip, so he found a local bar and ordered up a shot of whiskey. He realized too late that he should've brought his own small bottle of whiskey with him, but he hadn't thought of it at the time. He found a secluded corner in the bar, hiding in the murky shadows of a booth. He transferred the amber liquid into his Home Sweet Home shot glass and downed the whiskey.

Within moments, Jeff found himself back home, squatting in front of the shot glass display shelves. His body was in a crouched position because he had been sitting in a booth in the bar when he drank the shot, but he now had no seat beneath him. He fell back awkwardly to the floor, laughing. He would have to remember to drink the shots standing up from now on.

And then Jeff traveled. The Hawaii shot glass took him to Oahu. He found himself in Pearl Harbor, right near the USS Arizona memorial. On a whim, he took the boat shuttle to the USS Arizona Memorial, a floating memorial built over the sunken hull of the Battleship USS Arizona, the final resting place for many of the ship's crew. In the shrine room, a marble wall exhibited the names of the men who lost their lives on the Arizona during the Japanese attack on Pearl Harbor. He spent a few more hours on the island, just wandering around and taking in the sights, then teleported back home.

A few days later he took a quick jump to London where he strolled past the Tower of London. He visited the wax museum at Madame Tussauds; the replicas of the famous people inside were incredibly life-like and very creepy. Then a quick shot from the Home Sweet Home shot glass brought him right back to his house. Jeff remembered to bring his own whiskey with him this time. The Home Sweet Home shot glass worked perfectly every time. It brought him right back to the house, right back into his attic, right back in front of the shot glass display cabinet.

More traveling followed. Jeff sauntered for an hour through downtown Tokyo, taking in all the crazy neon sights. He spent a few hours in Cairo wandering through the Museum of Egyptian Antiquities. He saw the sun set in the Red Square in Moscow. He saw the sun rise in Sydney near the Sydney Opera House. He traveled quite a lot those first few weeks after his discovery.

Until he broke the Home Sweet Home shot glass in Los Angeles. Jeff cursed himself a damn fool every time he thought about it. He had just eaten a greasy, but spectacularly delicious, double burger from some burger joint on Wilshire Boulevard and his fingers were slippery. He fumbled with the shot glass and it slipped from his grip. He watched it tumble end over end towards the hard concrete, as if it were moving in slow motion. His mind screamed as the shot glass shattered against the stone ground. He stared at the broken pieces for a long moment. Then he dropped to his knees and grabbed at them, trying to figure out some way to put it back together. But he knew it was hopeless. The shot glass was shattered beyond repair.

He had to take a long plane flight home from California after that. Luckily, Nancy was out of town for a few days on a business trip so he didn't have to explain where he was. Thank God that hadn't happened in Moscow. How the hell would I have gotten home from there? I don't even have a passport. And how long would it have taken me to get home from there, or from Sydney or Egypt? He actually broke out into a cold sweat as the questions kept repeating themselves in his mind; there was no good answer to any of them.

Jeff decided to stop drinking from the shot glasses after that.

But only because he had come up with a much better use for them.

"Too bad about Wasim, huh?"

Jeff looked curiously at Kate. She was a pretty little thing in her early twenties with long blonde hair and a sweet smile. Her desk was decorated with all kinds of frogs, ceramic frogs, plastic frogs, a frog notepad, a frog coffee cup. Some people around the office called her the froggy lady, but Jeff thought it was all just damn cute. She worked in data processing in a different part of the building, but they still saw each other several times a day because that department was always crunching report numbers for him. He hated sitting at his desk all day, so he would get up and walk over to their area to tell the team what data points he needed for his latest project, instead of just emailing them all the time. It was a perfect excuse to get a few more eyefuls of Kate.

"He's on permanent R and R," Kate added.

Jeff kept the smile off his lips. "Really?"

"He had some kind of nervous breakdown."

"I hadn't heard."

Kate nodded. "Yeah, he can't remember how he got to Argentina. Took him months to get back. They said he was real lucky he had his wallet on him. His driver's license was the only thing that saved him. He finally found a consulate building and they helped him get home."

Jeff listened quietly. "He really has no idea how he got there?"

Kate shook her head. "Nope. He said he was here and then all of a sudden he was in Buenos Aires. He said a wolf nearly bit his face off." She laughed, then quickly covered her mouth. "Sorry, I shouldn't laugh." She looked at Jeff. "How can someone go to Argentina and not even remember how he got there? That's pretty strange, right?"

"Poor guy obviously needs a lot of help."

Kate nodded. "I don't think they're going to let him out for quite some time." She smiled at him. "Hey, congrats on that promotion. We should celebrate."

Jeff smiled back. "Yes, we should."

<hr>

"You went out with that bimbo again, didn't you?"

"Come on, Nancy, it's for work. I have to finish that Pendleton project by next week."

"I don't like you spending so much time with her. You should be spending more time with me."

Jeff looked at Nancy. She was definitely starting to put on more weight; he could see it in her cheeks. And her new close-cropped haircut just looked plain stupid. It made her head look like a fat orb with tiny blades of brown grass covering it. She had such an unpleasant scowl on her face. It really made her look unattractive. In fact, it made her look downright ugly, like some nasty old witch from a bad horror movie. The dark shadows the nearby lamp splattered across her face didn't help matters either. Jeff had a hard time remembering what he had seen in her. She held no attraction for him whatsoever now. He hated just being in the same room with her. He reached out for her hand, more out of the desire to avoid another ugly fight than to actually touch her. "I've got a lot more responsibility now. I have to get this work done."

"Whatever." She jerked her hand away from his. "I guess that's more important than me." She stormed off.

Jeff got up and chased after her. "Come on, baby, don't be mad at me. You like the extra money I'm making, don't you? Come on." He grabbed her and pulled her into his arms.

Nancy fought back, but not very hard, then settled into his embrace.

"Come on, let's both relax. Have a drink with me."

"Okay, you jerk. But just one."

"Sure. Just one."

Jeff stood naked before his shot glass collection. He had moved the display shelf out of the attic and mounted it on the wall in his living room. It looked great right next to his severely under-utilized book shelves. One slot held a plain, clear-glass shot glass, filling the space where the Home Sweet Home shot glass had resided before he broke it. One of the slots was currently empty on the second row, third slot in from the left.

Jeff glanced down at the shot glass in his hand. The Eiffel Tower was etched into the glass and a flourishing script font spelled out *Paris*, the word nearly encircling the entire shot glass. Nancy always said she wanted to see France. He had gotten so sick and tired of her anyway. It was much easier just to send her away than to deal with her emotional bullshit. And he knew everything would be so much quieter and calmer without her. Too bad she was naked when she went. He wondered how long it would take Nancy to get back home. He wondered if she would ever get back home at all.

Jeff shrugged and put the Paris shot glass back on the shelf into the one empty slot on the second row. He stared at his collection for a moment longer then turned away.

Kate was waiting for him.

"Nice game." Paul Norton wiped his towel across his forehead, wiping away the sheen of sweat. He was a handsome man in his early thirties, obviously in good shape with well-defined muscles in his arms and legs. A headband kept his blond hair out of his eyes.

Jeff stepped off the racquetball court, following closely behind Paul. Around them, the sounds of hard rubber balls pinging off the walls could be heard in the other racquetball courts that filled this area of the fitness facility.

"Maybe one of these days you'll beat me," Paul

said.

"But not today," Jeff said, cutting him off before Paul spoke the words he always spoke after he beat Jeff. "Yeah, I know."

Paul patted him on the shoulder. "Come on, being the second best racquetball player in the building is nothing to be ashamed about. You're getting better."

"You think so?" Jeff asked.

Paul nodded. "A little better every time."

"Hey, let's go to Heston's Pub and grab a drink. Whadya say?" Jeff said. He twirled his racquet in his hand.

Paul glanced up at the large clock on the wall. He looked back to Jeff. "Sure, okay, but just one. I gotta get home to take Paulie junior to his basketball game."

Jeff smiled and nodded. "Yeah, sure. Just one."

Jeff relaxed in his recliner in his living room and smiled. It was time to celebrate. He had a great new job. A great new girlfriend. He was the new reigning racquetball champion. Things were looking up for ol' Jeff Grandlin.

He poured himself a shot of whiskey. He raised the glass to his lips, but then stopped himself. He glanced at the shot glass. There were no markings on it. No city name. No graphic of any exotic destination. He smiled softly as he downed the shot.

He felt the familiar sensation immediately, the tingling in his limbs that signaled an imminent teleportation. No! Jeff glanced down at the glass. There was nothing on the glass. There was nothing!

How can I be about to teleport? There's nothing on the glass!

The tingling sensation continued to radiate along his limbs.

He looked back up at the display shelves. The shelving. Something about the shelving screamed at his mind. They were made of yew wood. The magic wood. And then he realized with a rising flood of panic the true implication of that fact. The yew wood held the magic. Yes, it was the whiskey that released it, but it was the yew wood that infused the shot glasses with their power. The prickling shivers reached his forearms and calves. Jeff stared down at the shot glass that had no destination etched into its glass, no city name painted on its side. Nothing.

Nowhere.

Jeff opened his fingers in horror and let the shot glass fall from his grip. The shot glass fell to the floor and rolled across the tiles, hitting the wall just beneath the display shelving. The shelving slots were full, expect for the one empty slot in the display case that had held the plain, clear-glass shot glass.

His fingers and toes tingled madly. His luck had just run out. Jeff didn't have time to scream before he vanished.

TERRORSTORY #24
THE CHAMPION

"**L**ook, if it isn't the King of the Farts!" Michael Tremayne bellowed. "How goes it in Stinkshire, Vaughn?"

Vaughn Gerhardt paused on the gravel path, a deep frown marring his otherwise attractive face. He was a wiry blond haired man, dressed in a tunic and breeches. Around them, the bustle of the Yorkshire Renaissance Faire was in full swing. About half of the people were dressed in jeans or shorts and t-shirts, while the other half of the faire guests were decked out in full medieval regalia, giving them the appearance of a noble lord or lady, a peasant, a brigand, a busty wench, or some other medieval

65

persona. Hundreds of people filled the outdoor food court area, carrying plates overflowing with vegetable tempura, enormous turkey legs, chicken pot pies, and bratwursts. Many a hand clutched a foamy beer. Nearby, some kids laughed as they played with the marshmallow catapults at a vendor's kiosk. A woman in a nearby booth dressed in a tight-fighting bodice called out to a passerby, entreating him to come play with her pickles.

"Lay off, Michael," Tory Wallace shot back. Tory was a pretty brunette, dressed in skin-tight black leggings and a laced-up leather top that showed plenty of cleavage. A sheathed rapier was stuck into her black leather belt. She stopped and stood before Michael, a frown tugging her lips down.

Vaughn stood silently next to Tory, glowering. "Come on," he said in a low voice. He tried to pull Tory away from Michael, but Tory remained where she was, her hands firmly planted on her hips.

"The only thing I'm going to lay is you after you dump that dreck," Michael said. He was a muscular man with a thick head of long flowing black hair that fell past his shoulders. He lifted his mug with a wildly exaggerated flourish and took a deep drink of his amber ale. His grey eyes were shiny and laced with streaks of red. Several attractive women sat at the table with him, and several other women stood nearby.

"The only thing you are going to lay is an egg," Tory shot back. "Oh, wait, it's already all over your face."

Michael raised his mug. "And we all know what's going to be all over face. It ain't gonna be no egg. It'll be thick and gooey, though. Just like you like it."

Several of the women gathered around Michael tittered.

Vaughn tugged on Tory's arm. "Come on, Tory."

Michael returned his attention to the bevy of beauties surrounding him. "You see, my dear wenches. Like I was saying before I was rudely interrupted by the presence of these mere mortals, those old knights of yesteryear don't have nothin' on me." He paused. "Why, if I was alive back then, I'd be ruling the jousts. Those poor sods wouldn't stand a chance against me in a tournament." He raised his mug and took a deep drink. "Not a chance."

"Come on, Tory. Let's go." This time Vaughn managed to pull the still-scowling Tory away from Michael, and they continued on their way.

Michael raised his mug, shouting after them. "Ha, another victory for me! Another opponent vanquished!"

❦

"Michael really thinks he's the best knight in the tournament. Can you believe it?" Vaughn said. A half-empty mug of ale rested on the wooden table before him. A nearly empty plate of fried vegetable tempura sat next to the mug, the greasy residue from the fried food staining the paper plate. Vaughn and Tory were sitting in the outdoor food court, near one of the stages. Behind them on the stage, a juggler dressed as a court jester was putting on his show. Laughter rippled through the crowd as the juggler pretended to burn his hands on the flaming batons he was juggling.

Tory waved her hand dismissively at Vaughn. "Michael knows it's all scripted by the story council," she said. "We just picked him randomly." A cloth bandanna was wrapped around the top of her head, keeping her long brunette hair from falling into her face. She adjusted the scabbard for the rapier she wore at her side, then sat down at the bench. A gigantic turkey leg rested on the table before her.

Vaughn nodded at Tory. "You know it and I know it, but Michael just doesn't get it. He really thinks he's the best. He thinks the story council chose him because he's the best." Vaughn paused. "He's such an insufferable ass now. Walking around boasting and bragging to everybody how much his mere presence in the jousts fills up the seats."

Tory looked over Vaughn's shoulder at something going on behind him. "He fills up a lot of things," she said around a mouthful of turkey meat.

Vaughn shifted his body to see what Tory was looking at, squeaking out a baby fart as he turned his body, and saw Michael Tremayne. The damn guy always seemed to be at the outdoor food court at the same time they were. They had just seen him yesterday, when Michael had hailed Vaughn as the king of the farts, and here he was again today. Several busty wenches surrounded Michael again, smiling at him, laughing at his witticisms. Michael stood with one knee on the wooden bench, his hand resting on the pommel of the sheathed sword that was strapped to his waist. He was damn handsome, Vaughn had to admit, with his long flowing black hair and his charming look-at-my-white-teeth smile. He heard Michael tell a busty wench with boobs about to burst forth from her tight bodice to fetch him a sassafras and she obediently scurried off to get him one. Vaughn looked back to Tory. "It doesn't help that they fawn all over him."

Tory looked at the entourage of admirers surrounding Michael, then back to Vaughn. She smiled knowingly. "Well, that pig is about to get a big surprise."

Vaughn looked at her curiously.

"We changed the script for the next tournament."

He waited for her to continue.

"I spoke to the story council and presented some new twists." Tory grabbed the turkey leg from her plate and pointed it at Vaughn. "*You* are going to be champion."

"Me? Are you serious?"

Tory took a big bite out of the turkey leg. "Yep. They agreed."

Vaughn looked over to Michael. "He's not going to be happy about that." Vaughn smiled. "He's not going to be happy about that at all."

Michael Tremayne stared at his opponent and laughed a scoffing laugh. "You fool, you have no chance against me." He sat atop his warhorse, fully armored for the joust, his helmet faceplate flipped up. The man facing him was nothing. Vaughn was a scrawny blond with a vulgar penchant for farting at the most inopportune times. His thick straw-colored hair was a draw to some of the women in the camp, but Michael thought he had too many freckles coloring his face. But who was he to judge what some ladies wanted. He had enough admirers to keep him content, and warm at night. He was the champion, after all. Vaughn could have all the leftovers he wanted.

This was the final joust of the tournament. Michael had already unseated Cavandish earlier in the day, so the fat man was out of the tournament. Vaughn had defeated Drake in a surprising victory. So now only he and Vaughn remained. The true champion versus the king of the farts.

The queen stepped onto the sand of the tilting yard. She was dressed in her full royal attire, her clothes thick and puffy around her body. She raised her hand to quiet the gathered crowd. The oval jousting arena was surrounded by eager guests filling the stands, all of them anxiously anticipating the battle that was about to begin. The queen addressed the two armored men on horseback before her. "My noble knights, are you ready to fight for your queen?" Her gaze moved from one man to the next.

"I am ready, my queen!" Michael shouted, his boisterous voice drowning out Vaughn's similar proclamation. Michael raised his gauntleted fist high. "I am ready to be your champion!"

The gathered crowd cheered.

"Let the joust begin!" the queen commanded.

Michael spurred his horse on, charging towards Vaughn. He lowered his lance, holding it tight against his side, pointing it straight towards his challenger.

Vaughn charged towards Michael, his lance lowered and ready to strike.

Michael struck Vaughn square in his shield, right between the eyes of the lion that was part of Vaughn's crest. The lance splintered under the force of his strike. The lance was already scored and weakened to shatter on impact, all part of the scripted show, so the explosion of wood splinters caught neither man off guard. Vaughn staggered in his saddle but stayed seated.

Whistling and cheering and hooting filled the jousting arena with empowering sounds. Michael loved those sounds. Every last whistle, every last clap. He loved them all. They gave him energy and strength. And they fed him. They fed his voracious, insatiable need for acclaim.

Michael's squire handed him a fresh lance as he returned to his side of the field. This was the killing round. Vaughn was supposed to hit him on the left side of his shield and he was supposed to tumble off his horse. Supposed to, was the operative phrase. Michael grinned darkly behind his faceplate. Supposed to. We'll just see about that, he thought. He scoffed inwardly. Did they really expect him to lose? Did they really expect him to just hand his title over to Vaughn? Oh, he had graciously accepted their script changes with a nod and a smile, but he had no intention of following them.

Michael spurred his horse forward, lowering the lance into position. Through the narrow slit in his visor, he could see Vaughn shifting his shield into position. Michael shifted his lance, zeroing in on Vaughn's shield, his intended scripted target. The horses thundered closer. At the last moment, Michael shifted his lance, tilting it up towards Vaughn's exposed left shoulder. The lance struck Vaughn's shoulder plate with a resounding crunch. The force of the blow spun Vaughn violently backwards and his body twisted hard in the saddle. He went tumbling to the ground, landing hard on his shoulder and neck.

Michael tossed his lance aside and quickly turned his horse to face Vaughn. All around him, the crowd went wild, cheering and whistling and clapping.

Vaughn staggered to his feet and stumbled in the sand. He grabbed at his shoulder. His squire raced up to him with his sword, but Vaughn brusquely waved him away with a curse. He stalked towards Michael, his plate armor clanking as he moved.

Michael dismounted. "Sword!" he shouted and held out his hand. Michael's squire raced towards him, the sword clutched to his chest. Michael took the offered sword from his squire and squared off to face Vaughn.

"What the fuck, Tremayne? You dislocated my shoulder," Vaughn said as he approached him. Vaughn's helmet visor was still down, so his words came out muted, but Michael still understood them all the same.

"Take your sword and fight me, fool," Michael said in a commanding tone.

"Fuck you. I'm supposed to win the tournament this time."

Michael put his sword to Vaughn's chest. "Yield."

Vaughn batted the sword away with his armored glove.

Michael raised his sword and brought the hard handle down on top of Vaughn's helmet. Vaughn staggered and dropped to his knees under the heavy blow. "Yield!" Michael shouted so the crowd could hear. "Yield to your champion!"

The crowd roared with laughter and whistles and cheers. Some boos and hisses filtered through the noise, but they were easily overpowered by the laughter and the cheers.

Vaughn shook his head, as if trying to clear his muddled thoughts from the blow he had just received. He said nothing.

Michael reached down and flipped up Vaughn's visor. He took a step back and raised his sword, pointing the sharp tip straight at Vaughn's exposed face. "Yield or die!"

The crowd roared and whistled and cheered even louder.

Vaughn glared at Michael.

Michael lowered his voice so only Vaughn could hear him. "Yield or I *will* kill you."

"You're crazy. You're a goddamned lunatic."

Michael inched the blade closer to his face. "Yield."

"I yield, you fuck."

"Louder."

"I yield!" Vaughn shouted.

Michael stepped back and lowered his sword. He turned to face the queen and the royal court. He thrust his sword upwards in victory. The deafening cheers from the ground fueled Michael's admiration. For himself. He was the greatest champion the tournament had ever seen. No one could defeat him.

⋘◦◦●◦◦⋙

From the outside, the shop looked like a typical vendor's stall at the Yorkshire Renaissance Faire, with its name — All Things Magikal — carved into a wooden sign that hung above its wide opening. It was flanked by a wooden sword and shield vendor on the left, and a pewter vendor on the right filled with tiny sculptures of dragons, goblets, and pewter chess sets featuring wizards and knights. What set All Things Magikal slightly apart from the other shops was the row of black and silver beaded curtains hanging in front of its doorway, hiding its interior from the casual passerby.

Vaughn and Tory climbed the few wooden steps that led up to the shop's entrance and pushed through the beaded curtains. The interior was dim and cool, a nice respite from the hot sunny day outside. They had some time to kill before the next joust, so they decided to go browsing through some shops. Grotesque masks with faces that had enormous crooked noses and twisted mouths adorned part of one wall. A few skulls were snared in a web of ropes that dangled down from a ceiling cross beam. Deeper into the shop, several glass-topped counters lined the walls, their interiors filled with all manner of dried herbs, amulets, and vials. Numerous other visitors to the faire were in the shop. Many were dressed in medieval character attire, while some were dressed in normal civilian jeans and t-shirts. A couple in pirate costumes browsed through a nearby bin of medieval magic tricks.

Vaughn picked up a golden amulet from a table filled with jewelry. The amulet had a jousting knight etched into its shiny surface.

"Damn it, did you fart?" Tory wrinkled her noise.

"Sorry, it was that greasy turkey leg."

The beads made a jangling noise and Vaughn looked up to see Michael striding into the shop. Vaughn quickly put the amulet down and grabbed Tory's arm, herding her away from the doorway, moving deeper into a darker corner of the shop.

74

"What?" Tory asked.

Vaughn shushed her. "It's Michael," he whispered.

"Okay, so? Why are we hiding? We should confront his ass."

Vaughn looked up at her, feeling his face redden. "No, not now."

"You can be a real wuss, sometimes," Tory said to him, joining in his conspiratorial whisper.

"Me? You and your story council didn't do anything, either. You just let it slide."

"I told you I filed a protest. The others overrode it. They said that was one of the greatest jousts we've ever had at the faire. It's going to bring in hundreds of new paying customers. Maybe even thousands. People are still talking about it. They are going to come to see Michael."

"He damn near killed me."

"Oh, come on. You're exaggerating."

Vaughn frowned. "He threatened to kill me, Tory."

"And yet here you still stand."

"Yeah, I guess me almost dying is worth good word of mouth for the faire." His tone was clearly sarcastic. Vaughn looked away from Tory. He absently rubbed at his sore shoulder. It turned out it wasn't dislocated, but it still hurt like hell even days later.

They both watched Michael. He clearly had not come to browse. He moved straight for the back counter where a large elderly woman was seated in a chair behind it. She was dressed in a flowing medieval dress, a sash of golden thread tied about her waist. "Is it ready?" Michael asked her.

The shopkeeper nodded. She disappeared into the

back room, moving past a black curtain that separated the back area from the rest of the shop.

Michael turned from the counter to glance about the shop. Vaughn and Tory both quickly turned their backs to him, pretending to study the stone statues of gargoyles that filled the corner of the shop.

"Here you are," they heard the shopkeeper say as she stepped back out from behind the black curtains.

Vaughn chanced a furtive glance over at Michael to see him taking a small vial from the shopkeeper.

"It's stronger this time?" Michael asked.

The shopkeeper nodded. "Quite strong. Use it sparingly on those poor girls."

Michael handed the shopkeeper some money and she rang up the sale.

Vaughn and Tory watched Michael leave the shop.

"Did you hear what she said? Use it sparingly on those poor girls. That's disgusting." Vaughn frowned. "What the hell did she give him? Some kind of magic love potion?"

※─≪☀≫─※

Vaughn and Tory followed Michael. And Vaughn's fears turned out to be well founded. They saw Michael pour a drop of the liquid he had purchased from All Things Magikal into a woman's goblet, making sure she wasn't looking when he did it. Within minutes, the woman was fawning all over him, blatantly rubbing her breasts against him as she caressed Michael's inner thigh with great enthusiasm.

"Okay, that's it," Tory fumed. "You were right about that pig." She started to storm towards Michael, her face laced with disgust. "He needs to be stopped."

Vaughn grabbed Tory's arm, stopping her. "No, wait. I have a better idea."

Vaughn entered All Things Magikal and walked briskly over to the shopkeeper. Tory followed on his heels. They had argued about filing a complaint against Michael and the shopkeeper, but Vaughn had convinced Tory to try his approach first. They would use the shop's power against Michael. If that didn't teach him a lesson, then they would go to the Faire authorities and turn both Michael and the shopkeeper in.

The elderly woman looked up at Vaughn as he approached her, but said nothing.

"Do you have something that will make a wish come true?" Vaughn asked.

The shopkeeper looked curiously at him.

"Not mine," Vaughn said. He motioned to Tory as she moved up to his side. "Not ours. Someone else's."

"You want it for a friend," the shopkeeper said.

Vaughn nodded at the woman. "Yes. For a very dear friend."

"Come on, Vaughn. That's just silly," Tory said. "You realize you paid two hundred bucks for a piece of costume jewelry, right?"

"Is it? You saw what effect that stuff she gave Michael had on that woman. It was immediate. She probably would have done him right then and there if he had asked her to."

Tory shook her head. "That doesn't mean this will work. That shopkeeper probably just gave Michael some super Spanish Fly or something."

"Maybe," Vaughn said. "But I think that shop really does have magical powers. There's been too many stories about people visiting that store and weird things happening."

Tory said nothing.

Vaughn held up the gold chain and dangled the amulet in front of Tory. It was the golden amulet that had a jousting knight etched into its shiny surface that he had looked at earlier. The shopkeeper from All Things Magikal had enchanted it. She had disappeared behind the black curtain for a few moments and then stepped back into the shop with a knowing smile. It would grant the wearer's deepest wish, she told them. It was good for one wish, the shopkeeper had said. After that, the amulet would lose all its power and just become a decorative piece of gold.

"You actually believe it has some power?" Tory asked. "It's just a piece of metal. It's probably not even real gold."

Vaughn fingered the amulet and looked up at Tory. "You don't believe in magic? You don't believe there's a power greater than us?"

"Maybe. I just don't think that woman in All Things Magikal has the ability to tap into it." Tory shrugged. "I believe what I can see and what I can feel."

"What about what you can smell?"

Tory froze for just a quick second, then wrinkled her nose and waved her hand frantically in front of her face. "Son of a bitch, Vaughn. That's just nasty."

Vaughn grinned. He continued to rub his fingers

over the golden amulet.

"Why don't you wear it?" Tory said. "Why don't you see if it grants you your deepest wish."

Vaughn shook his head. "No way. Those things always backfire. Always. They never turn out well for the wisher."

"So you think Michael's deepest wish will backfire on him?"

"That's what I'm hoping."

Tory looked at Vaughn for a moment. She leaned in and kissed his cheek. "You *do* have a little nasty in you. I like that."

Vaughn kept his expression even.

"So what do you think Michael's deepest wish is?"

Vaughn shrugged. "I don't know. I just know whatever it is, it won't end up like he expects it to."

"You think he's actually going to wear that?" Tory asked.

"Sure. If the queen presents it to him after the next joust." He paused and looked at Tory. "I mean, he is scripted to win again, isn't he?"

Tory looked away sheepishly.

Michael fingered the golden amulet hanging from the golden chain around his neck, studying the engraving of the jousting knight that was etched into its surface. The queen had presented it to him after a well-fought victory against Drake. He sat in his tent, resting on the throne-like chair he had custom made for himself. He draped his leg over the side of the throne, absently taking a drink from a silver goblet. He truly was a great champion. If only he could have lived in those medieval times. He would have ruled the tournaments. No one would be able to defeat him. Michael felt himself stiffen. No woman would be able to resist him. He closed his eyes, his fingers caressing the jousting knight amulet. If only.

⧫⬥⬥⬥⧫

When Michael Tremayne opened his eyes again, he was no longer sitting on his throne. He was no longer in his tent. He felt odd, almost disembodied. What a strange feeling, he thought. He couldn't feel his arms or his legs. This is a crazy dream, he thought.

His vision seemed strange, too. It was as if he were absorbing the events happening around him, but not really seeing them. It was a very odd feeling that he couldn't explain. A very uncomfortable feeling. He was in the middle of a tilting yard where jousts were held. He could see fully armored knights trotting their steeds about the dusty field. He could see men dressed in tunics, practicing their swordplay just beyond the field. Not really see, but he could sense them all around him as if he had a full circle field of vision. He was back in medieval England. Michael didn't know how or why, but he just knew that's where he was. That's *when* he was.

A knight charged towards him, his sword raised high and ready to strike. Michael could feel the ground trembling as the horse's hooves pounded over the dirt. Again, it was on odd feeling because he didn't have any sensation of actually having any legs, but he could still feel the ground vibrating beneath him.

The knight raced closer, his face tight, his lips

curled into a snarl.

Michael mentally screamed at himself to move, but he couldn't. He was immobile.

The charging knight loomed closer. The knight narrowed his eyes and reared back for the strike. His sword gleamed in the hot sunlight.

Michael could not move no matter how much his mind was screaming at himself to get out of the way of the charging knight.

The sword came slashing down in a vicious blow. A loud thunk filled the jousting field.

And he felt it. Michael felt the strike of the sword as if the blade was cutting through his flesh. But he had no flesh. He had no body. Despite his lack of skin and bone, an intense pain exploded through him.

The knight circled his horse around to charge at him again. The sword flashed hotly and another loud wooden thunk rang out.

Michael felt excruciating pain radiate through his mind. He realized with growing terror exactly what was happening. The wooden thunk echoed through his mind. He was no longer a man. He no longer had a human body. He was a quintain. He was a wooden dummy the knights practiced their jousting techniques on. He was trapped inside a block of wood and straw in the shape of a man.

Michael wanted to laugh, but he had no voice. He had the biggest wood in all of England between his legs. He was the center of attention. He would never be defeated.

Another knight charged towards Michael, his gleaming sword raised.

Michael wanted to scream, but he had no mouth.

Vaughn took his victory lap around the jousting field, his sword raised high. Michael had been right about one thing — it was great to be the champion. The cheers from the crowd were music to his ears. Vaughn lifted his butt off the saddle and squeaked out a fart.

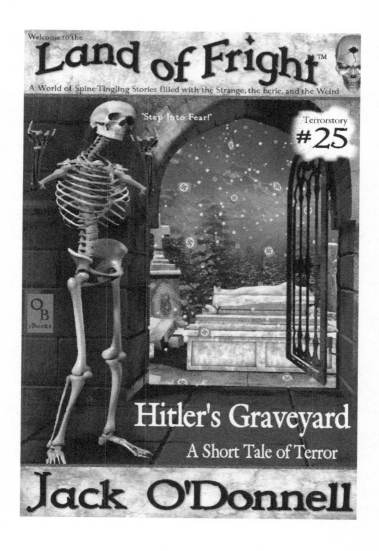

TERRORSTORY #25
HITLER'S GRAVEYARD

World War II
Somewhere in the Hurtgen Forest
December 1944

He had been dead for more than thirty-six hours but his jutting penis was still as stiff as a board. The corpse lay on a table that was set up right before a shallow empty grave. Nine naked German soldiers stood off to the side of the grave. They all stood at rigid attention, their expressions blank, their skin very pale, nearly blue. The bitter afternoon cold did not affect them. Snow blanketed the ground within, and around, the entire cemetery. Beyond the cemetery, fir trees that towered seventy to a hundred feet into the sky encircled the graveyard.

"No wonder they called him a hero," Helena Schmidt said coyly, admiring the corpse's large erection. She was a nurse, a pretty young German woman with golden hair and blue eyes. She was dressed in a thick white parka, the hood lined with thick fox fur. She reached out and stroked the dead man, running her slender fingers up and down the hard shaft. "Ooooh," she murmured, "it's so cold." A white wispy cloud of her breath glistened in the afternoon air as she exhaled.

"He's been on ice for a few days. What do you expect?" Oberleutnant Gruber looked at the petite young woman disdainfully. Gruber was a stout German man, with a broad chest and a broad face. He had glacial blue eyes and a wide mouth. He, too, was dressed in a thick white parka. A Karabiner 98k rifle was strapped around his shoulder.

"Perhaps you'd like to take him for one last ride, Helena?" the man next to the young German nurse inquired hopefully. He was Doctor Melange. His deep set black eyes were wide with eagerness in the afternoon chill. His tone was obvious and direct. There was no question that Dr. Melange wanted Helena to take him up on the offer, and that he would be more than willing to watch. He was dressed in a long white overcoat, his hands covered in black gloves.

Helena turned to the doctor and slapped him playfully, but hard, on the cheek. "You are a nasty man," she told him.

Hauptmann Ernst Frankel strode out of the small building behind them and moved quickly over to them. Frankel was dressed in a long, winter camouflage overcoat. He had a strong face, with prominent cheekbones and a square chin with a deep cleft carved into it. Frankel glanced down at the corpse that rested on the table before the empty grave. "Is this him?"

Oberleutnant Gruber nodded.

Hauptmann Frankel turned back to the building from where he had just come, raised his hand and waved his long, thin fingers in the air.

Four uniformed German soldiers emerged from the dark shadows, two of them clutching a naked man between them. The naked man was an American GI captured days earlier in the intense fighting in the Hurtgen Forest.

Dr. Melange nodded as he studied the physique of the naked POW. He circled the American, his gaze covering the man's body from his head to his feet. The doctor's head bobbed up and down approvingly. The prisoner was obviously a fresh recruit the Americans had just brought in to reinforce their positions in the Hurtgen forest, and had only been recently captured; the bitter cold and deleterious fighting conditions still hadn't drained the captive of his health and vitality. The prisoner shivered, but said nothing as the doctor continued to study him. "Yes, good." The doctor then pointed to the corpse on the table. "Put him in."

Frankel nodded at the two other German soldiers who were not gripping the prisoner. The two German soldiers lifted the corpse up from the table and shuffled towards the open grave. One of the soldiers nearly lost his grip on the dead body, but quickly recovered.

"Gently! Gently!" Dr. Melange barked with a scolding tone. "He's already been battered enough."

The German soldiers finished placing the dead man into the shallow grave and stepped back. Helena stepped up to the grave and produced a penny postcard from somewhere inside her parka. It was a thin card with a black and white sketch portrait of the dead man in the grave on the face of the card. She turned the card over and read its contents. "Major Helmut Schossenfiel. Knights Cross recipient. Fallschirmjaeger." Helena turned the card back over to look at the striking black and white portrait of the Major. The Knights Cross medal was clearly visible in the portrait sketch, drawn on his uniform collar just below his neck.

"A true hero of the Reich," Dr. Melange said.

Helena bent down and gently set the penny postcard on the dead man's bare chest.

Dr. Melange turned to Frankel. "Bring the offering closer."

Frankel nodded at his two soldiers clutching the naked POW. The two German soldiers dragged the American over to the side of the grave. Frankel looked back over to the doctor. "Are we ready?"

Dr. Melange nodded.

Frankel motioned to his soldiers to begin.

Suddenly, a yellow liquid splashed onto the corpse, washing away some of the specks of dirt on the dead man's face with the force of the stream. The American POW looked at the Germans surrounding him and grinned a toothy grin as he continued to urinate on the dead German in the grave.

Gruber quickly drew his Luger and shot the prisoner in the head. The bullet jerked the American's head back sharply as fluids, bones, and bits of brain exploded out of the back of his skull.

"No!" Dr. Melange shouted. "I needed that man's blood!"

The POW fell backwards to the ground, the blood spilling out of him darkening the snow around his fallen body.

"Filthy pig," Gruber snarled down at the dead POW. He stepped up to the dead American and fired a point-blank shot into his chest.

Frankel frowned. He studied Gruber for a long moment. "Put that away, Oberleutnant," he said. Frankel's voice was calm, but laced with menace.

Gruber obeyed, holstering his weapon.

"Do we have any other prisoners on hand?" Dr. Melange asked.

"No," Frankel said. "He was the last." He stared disapprovingly at Gruber.

"There are more being brought in," Gruber said quickly. "The wagons should be here soon."

"Wagons?" Frankel frowned. "Is this what the great German Army has descended to? Needing to use horse-drawn wagons to move prisoners and supplies around?"

No one had any answers to his questions.

Frankel drew his Luger. He raised the weapon up and pointed it directly at Gruber's head. Gruber did not flinch; the Oberleutnant stared straight into the dark barrel of Hauptmann Frankel's weapon. Frankel then swung the gun towards the young nurse. "Use hers."

Helena took a step back, fear filling her face.

"No!" Dr. Melange shouted.

Frankel turned to see Dr. Melange shake his head

sharply.

"It needs to be a man's blood," the doctor said. "Man for man. Woman for woman. It is how it must be."

Frankel looked at Gruber, then at his four soldiers. They were valuable, trusted men. But this was the future of the Reich at stake. If this procedure continued to work as well as they had hoped, the German Army would be unstoppable. They would be able to resurrect every great hero who had been lost and send them back into battle. No, too much was at stake to worry about the life of one normal man. Frankel nodded to the two men standing near Gruber. The two soldiers moved quickly, grabbing Gruber and pinning his arms tight to his side.

Gruber looked up calmly at Frankel. "There is no need for this, Hauptmann. I will give myself to the Reich willingly."

The two German soldiers clutching Gruber looked at Frankel. Frankel gave a slight nod of his head and the soldiers released Gruber. Gruber looked at Frankel, a calm resolve coming over his face. "If you ever see my wife and children, tell them I love them."

Frankel nodded. He holstered his Luger.

Gruber moved to his knees and bowed his head over the grave, positioning himself over the corpse of Major Schossenfiel.

One of the German soldiers produced a Hitler youth knife and ran the sharp blade across Gruber's throat. Gruber gurgled, but otherwise made no sound as his life drained out of him. Blood pooled into the grave, spilling onto the dead man, covering his corpse in a thin coating of red. The two soldiers held Gruber's body over the grave, directing his blood to spill into the shallow carving cut into the earth where their dead hero lay.

"Cover the grave," Dr. Melange ordered as the last of the blood drained out of Gruber. "Quickly now. Quickly."

The four German soldiers covered the grave, shoveling dirt over the corpse with great efficiency. Within moments, the body was blanketed with a layer of graveyard dirt.

Dr. Melange, Helena, Hauptmann Frankel, and his four men stood at the side of the grave, watching, waiting. Blobs of white vapor oozed out of their noses and mouths as they breathed the cold air that filled the frigid forest. Gruber's drained dead body lay on its side near the grave, now forgotten.

The nine naked Germans stood silently nearby, still standing rigidly at attention. None of them turned their heads to watch what was happening only a few yards away from them. None of them oozed any whiteness from their noses or mouths. None of them needed to take a breath ever again.

"Just one, Sarge?" Private Leo Kern held up the lone cigarette that Sergeant Thomas Conner had just given him. Kern was a chubby kid with a red patch of hair on his head and a smattering of freckles dotting his face. He hadn't had enough time to get into decent shape before the Army shipped him off to the front lines.

Conner paused halfway out of the foxhole and glanced back at the portly private over his shoulder. A very light fog swirled around Conner, the white mist oozing down the sides of the hole to coat the bottom of the foxhole with a thin layer of roiling white haze. "If you're still here in the morning, I'll give you another one." Conner was a lean Irishman, with a small nose and a soft rounded jaw. His eyes were full of strength that contrasted sharply against the apparent weakness of his slim and slender body. He was small, but he was tough.

Kern frowned. "What's that supposed to mean?"

Conner sighed, exhaling a thin puff of white vapor, and moved back down into the foxhole next to Kern. "It means that if a Kraut patrol hasn't taken you as a prisoner in the hopes of torturing information out of you, or if they haven't put a few rounds through your skull, or if they haven't blown you to smithereens with mortars, then I'll give you another smoke tomorrow." He patted Kern on the shoulder. "Clear now?"

Kern nodded hesitantly.

Conner turned and put his hand back on the dirt lip of the foxhole, getting ready to climb out. The trees were so thick around them in the forest that even during the day the high midday sun could barely penetrate down to the spongy brown needles and decaying remnants of trunks and branches that littered the forest floor amidst the pockets of snow. The nights were worse, even darker, gloomier, the air itself turning thicker with an extra coating of hopelessness.

"Sarge?"

Conner paused again, but did not turn to face Kern.

"I don't have a light."

Conner sighed. He glanced up at the heavy growth

of trees blanketing the afternoon sky above him. Their vast canopy shadowed the world with an eerie twilight murkiness. The dense conifer forest was nearly impassable, thick with trees that made it difficult to move vehicles through the terrain, so much of the fighting was bitter close combat. Conner had been in the Ardennes for weeks now, leading a squad of eight men in nightly patrols near the German's front lines in the Hurtgen Forest, and there didn't seem to be any end to that duty in sight. Day after day it was the same. Send out a patrol. Fill up a few body bags. Get some fresh meat. Send out another patrol. Fill up more body bags. Now they were sending him recruits without their own smokes. Without even a damn lighter. Pretty soon Conner knew they would be sending him recruits without ammunition.

"Sarge?"

"Yeah, yeah. I heard you the first time." Conner dug into the pocket of his jacket and pulled out a lighter. It was the one Norris had loaned him after they liberated St. Lo in France. He rolled it though his fingers. It had a picture of a pretty French girl wearing a frilly skirt and holding a frothy mug of beer on one side. He had promised to give it back to Norris. Conner turned and tossed it to Kern. Dead men didn't have much use for lighters.

"Make sure you get down low and cup your hands over the flame," Conner warned. "All it takes is one flash of light for the Krauts to draw a bead on you and we'll have artillery shells in our faces all night."

Kern nodded. "Sarge?"

Conner waited for him to continue.

"Thanks for saving my life yesterday." Kern

hesitated, then glanced down away from Conner. "And the day before that."

"No sweat, kid. I just expect you to do the same for me some day. Then we'll call it even."

Kern nodded. "What... what do I do if I see some Kr... Germans?"

"Kill them."

"Kill them?" Kern asked, a hesitant, wondering tone evident in his question.

Conner stared hard at the private. "Did I miss something? Is the war over? Did we win?"

"No... no..."

Conner pointed to the Thompson submachine gun resting near the wall of the foxhole. "Did they show you how to use that?"

Kern followed his pointing finger and stared at the submachine gun as if he had just seen it for the first time. "Once," he finally said. "I was trained more with the Garand than that, but that's what they gave me."

"Pick it up."

Kern slid his cigarette behind his ear, pocketed the lighter in his jacket, and then picked up his weapon. He looked up at Conner expectantly. Suddenly, Kern whipped the submachine gun around in front of him and pulled the trigger. A dozen rounds spit out of the muzzle, the rat-at-tat deafening in the silence, the sound ricocheting of the thick growth of fir trees that surrounded them.

"What the fuck are — " Conner shut his mouth quickly as the dirt a few feet away from his head exploded into the air in half a dozen tiny eruptions. He spun and brought his M1 carbine to bear as he saw the dark shapes looming up out of the murky shadows of the forest. He fired at the approaching Germans, taking one enemy soldier down with a few quick shots across his knees, then another German with a few bullets across his chest. Conner could make out a dozen more shapes in the distance, and maybe even a dozen more beyond that. They were making a push. The damned Germans were trying to take their positions.

Gunfire erupted all around them. Wood cracked and splintered as bullets slammed into tree trunks and tree limbs. Men howled and screamed all around them. More guns blazed.

"Let's go!" Conner grabbed Kern by the collar of his jacket and yanked the private to the edge of the foxhole. "They're making a push. Let's get the hell out of here."

The two men scrambled out of the foxhole, racing back towards the rear of the American position. Conner leaped over a protruding tree trunk, pulling Kern over the massive limb with a hard tug.

Bullets whizzed past all around them.

The cigarette Kern had lodged behind his ear dropped to the floor of the forest, immediately disappearing into a patch of white snow, but Kern didn't notice. He just kept running, keeping as close to Conner as he could, clutching his Thompson tight.

Snow crunched and branches snapped and cracked beneath their boots as the two soldiers ran. The fog thickened around them, billowing out from beneath their boots with each running step they took. A shrill whistle suddenly filled the forest.

"Incoming!" Conner shouted.

A mortar exploded a dozen yards to their right, exploding up in the trees, sending hot shards of wood and razor-tipped splinters of bark hurtling in every direction.

Kern immediately dove to the ground, spreading himself prostrate on the carpet of snow and fir needles, putting his hands over his helmeted head. Conner grabbed him roughly by his jacket collar, yanking him back to his feet. "Grab a tree!" he ordered.

Kern turned terrified eyes to his sergeant. "What?"

Conner shoved him towards a large trunk. "Hug that fucker like you wanna do her all night long," he commanded. Conner moved to a tree near Kern and quickly practiced what he had just preached. He slung his M1 back over his shoulder and wrapped his arms around the tree, clinging tightly to it, moving himself to face the direction of the barrage, keeping the wide trunk between himself and the German artillery. He ducked his head down to his shoulder as another shrill whistle filled the air.

Kern listened to the incoming mortar shell, the whistling coming closer, coming in fast. KRAAACK! The tops of half a dozen trees not more than a few yards from their position exploded into a torrent of shattered branches. Kern hugged his tree, keeping his head down. He watched with morbid fascination as a score of jagged chunks of tree slammed into the dirt where he had been laying not more than a few minutes ago, spearing the earth near his dropped submachine gun. He looked over at Conner with wide, fear-struck eyes.

"Let's go!" Conner urged. Conner pushed himself off the tree, unshouldered his carbine, and charged off.

Kern snatched his Thompson off the forest floor

and followed in hot pursuit.

They quickly reached another foxhole and jumped in. It was empty. The two recruits Conner had assigned to the hole before going to check on Kern were gone. He couldn't remember their names. He couldn't even remember what they looked like right now.

In the distance, more gunfire sounded. Mortars whistled in and exploded. Then more gunfire rang out.

"Where'd they go?" Kern asked, fingering his submachine gun nervously. He glanced around the area, but saw no movement in the dark growth of trees.

Conner noticed a splattering of blood on the edge of the foxhole, but said nothing about it to Kern. "I don't know," he said. "Right now it doesn't matter. We need to get back to base camp and tell the lieutenant the Krauts are making a big push."

"Don't you think he's figured it out by now?"

Conner ignored Kern's wisecrack and clambered out of the hole. "Let's go." But suddenly he paused, standing motionless as he stared into a wall of pure white fog. The white cloud was everywhere, in front of them, behind them, rising as high as the low tree branches. Visibility was beyond poor. Conner could barely make out his hand in front of his face. He could feel the fog curling about his legs as if it had an eerie, physical serpentine substance to it.

"What the hell is this?" Kern muttered.

"Welcome to the Hurtgen fucking forest," Conner commented flatly.

"Which way?" Kern asked.

Conner motioned straight ahead with his M1

carbine. "This way."

"You sure?"

"You wanna wait here and see if it clears?"

Kern stood quietly for a moment, then stepped past Conner, moving in the direction the sergeant had indicated.

Suddenly, three figures burst out of the fog, charging right at them. Before either man had a chance to fire his weapon, they were all on the ground, a tangle of flailing arms and wildly kicking legs. Chunks of snow and fir needles flew in all directions.

"Fuckin' A!" someone shouted. "It's the Sarge!"

Conner disentangled himself from the mass of bodies and quickly realized that the three figures were more of his men. Corporal Matthew Palinski, and Privates Vincenzo Scorelli and George Duff.

"What's going on, Sarge?" Corporal Palinski asked. Palinski was a wiry Pole with a long, narrow face and blue eyes. He had a light scar on his forehead where a bullet had grazed his flesh weeks earlier.

"The Germans are making a push. We need to get back to base," Conner answered.

"That's where we were headed," Scorelli told him. Private Scorelli was a short Italian with jet black hair. He had a round face and a pug nose that had been broken more than once in his twenty years of life. His eyes were a dark brown that nearly matched the color of his heavy boots.

"Score, you dumb ass," Kern scolded the little Italian. "You're going the wrong way."

"Like hell," Scorelli said. "You guys are going the wrong way. Two Panzers and a shitload of trigger-happy Krauts are right over that ridge." Scorelli pointed back in the direction they had come, back toward a rising slope in the distance that was barely visible in the thick, shifting fog.

"Yeah, well, a dozen Germans are probably about a hundred yards behind us, if not less," Kern responded.

"Panzers? You sure?" Conner asked Scorelli.

"They sure looked like fucking Panzers to me," Scorelli said. "So much for no tanks in this fucking forest."

"Shit," Duff said softly. "Shitty shit shit." Private Duff was a tall young man in his early twenties, with long gangly arms. He had a soft, effeminate face, a face obviously not used to the harsh conditions he found himself in.

Everyone turned to look at Duff. Duff glanced at them, then back at the surrounding dark mass of trees that encircled them before returning their gazes. "We're surrounded," Duff added just as softly.

Everyone was quiet for a long moment.

"Fuck," Scorelli finally muttered. He drummed his fingers on the handle of his Colt M1911 that was shoved into his belt at his waist.

After another moment of uncomfortable silence, Conner felt everyone's gazes turn to stare at him.

Suddenly, behind his men, Conner saw the fog shift to reveal the outline of what looked like some kind of building in the distance. He motioned quickly for everyone to get down with a few quick short chops of his hand. The others quietly obeyed his silent command. They turned to follow his gaze.

"Somebody get out their map," Conner whispered.

Duff quickly obliged, pulling his silk map out of his jacket pocket. The map was printed on a silky, waterproof material to help preserve it and prolong its lifespan. It showed the most prominent features of the Hurtgen forest and surrounding towns.

The fog swirled, revealing another building beyond the first, then another beyond that. Even farther in the distance, Conner thought he saw what appeared to be a cemetery filled with white crosses. A large mausoleum sat off to the right of several rows of tombstones. "Do you know where we are?" Conner asked of Duff.

"Yeah, right here." Duff put his finger on the map. "Just about smack dab in the middle of the forest. I verified our position with the lieutenant last night."

Conner nodded. "Okay, what town is that?"

Duff was quiet for a moment. Conner turned to see him studying the map intently. "Duff, what town is that?" he repeated.

Duff slowly looked up from the silk drawing. "Sarge, that town ain't on the map."

"What do you mean it's not on the map?" Conner asked. "It's gotta be on the map."

"And the Germans are history, right, Sarge? They don't have enough men or materials to make a push. We already won the war." Scorelli held out his Garand rifle to Conner. "Sir, I'd like to turn in my weapon. Book me on the next boat home."

Conner silenced Scorelli with a glare. He looked back toward the structures, catching fleeting glimpses of buildings, the graveyard.

"I don't like the looks of this, Sarge," Kern muttered as he peered through the murky white haze.

"I don't like the looks of you," Scorelli taunted. "Your legs look like you're standing on a big vat of jello. I ain't seen so much quiverin' in my life."

"Fuck you, Scorelli," Kern said. "Why you always have to be an asshole?"

"I don't know," Scorelli said. "Why you always look so stupid? Maybe we was just both born this way."

As always, Conner ignored their quips. He looked at the young men around him. "Let's go." Conner took one slow, cautious step after the next, his rifle held ready at his waist, the weapon leading the way.

"Man, it's quiet," Palinski said. "I don't hear any shooting any more."

No one said anything to that. It was true. The forest was very quiet all around them. They headed deeper into the fog, their booted feet crunching softly in the snow as they walked. They moved slowly closer towards the cemetery that floated in and out of visibility amidst the white mist.

⊰⊱⊰⊱⊰⊱

The dirt covering the grave moved. Then it moved again, shifting even more. A hand appeared from beneath the dirt, the fingers curling and uncurling as they broke the surface.

Hauptmann Frankel looked on in awe as a dark shape rose up out of the grave before them.

"Welcome back to the war, Major," Dr. Melange said as the newly risen man stood tall to his full height.

Helena stepped forward and lovingly began wiping away the dirt and blood from the resurrected form of Major Helmut Schossenfiel.

"Is everybody seeing what I'm seeing?" Conner asked, his voice a low whisper. They were hidden behind a thick growth of underbrush on the edge of the cemetery. They had stopped at the border of the cemetery to scout their surroundings before going in. Conner could make out five German soldiers, a possible civilian, and what looked like a blonde woman standing around a gravesite.

Nine naked men stood off to the side of the grave. Conner frowned as he studied them for a moment. None of them moved. The others he saw standing around the grave exhaled cold puffs of air, but these nine did not even appear to be breathing at all. Then he saw the corpses laying prone around the gravesite. He counted ten bodies near the grave and an eleventh body sprawled several feet away from the grave site. His frown deepened. What the fuck was going on here?

"Yeah," Scorelli replied in a whisper. "We see it, but what the hell are we lookin' at?"

They watched with fascinated dread as a man climbed up out of the ground. Dirt spilled off the naked man's chest. They heard the man in the white overcoat wearing black gloves speak in German. His voice traveled clearly in the cold quiet of the cemetery.

"Anybody understand what he said?" Conner whispered.

Duff nodded. "He said '*Welcome back to the war, Major.*'"

"Welcome back to the war?" Conner echoed.

"Yes."

"*Back* to the war?"

"That's what he said, Sarge," Duff replied, keeping his voice very low.

The American soldiers watched as the blonde woman stepped up to the man who had just risen out of the grave and started wiping the blood and dirt off of him. She lingered on his large erection, wiping at it slowly.

"Jesus, look at the size of that prick," Scorelli muttered. "And I mean him *and* his cock."

The German officer stepped up to the newly risen naked man, motioning for the blonde woman to step aside. She moved away as the German officer drew his Luger and fired point blank range into the naked man's chest. The force of the bullet knocked the naked man back a step, but he stayed on his feet. There was no blood where the bullet had entered the naked man, nor any blood where it had exited his body.

"What the hell?" Palinski muttered.

The German officer nodded, clearly satisfied at what had just transpired, and holstered his weapon.

The blonde woman grabbed the naked man by the hand and led him towards a small stone building nearby. The naked man obediently followed the woman's lead, his first few steps awkward and fumbling but then becoming more assured and confident the more he moved. The four German soldiers and the civilian man followed the woman into the building as she guided the naked man inside.

The German officer barked a command at the nine other naked men and they followed him inside, shuffling their bare feet as they moved wordlessly through the snow.

Soon, the cemetery was empty of movement and quiet again. The corpses still littered the snow-covered ground, but they were frozen in death and lay unmoving.

"What the fuck?" Palinski muttered. "Sarge, what the hell are they doing? He just shot that guy point blank in the chest and he didn't go down."

"There wasn't any blood," Kern muttered. "He shot him and there wasn't any blood."

Scorelli shook his head. "There's no fucking way. That is not possible."

They were all quiet for a long moment, all of them staring at the vacated space, the empty grave, the corpses.

"It's Hitler's graveyard," Duff said, breaking the uneasy silence.

All the other men turned to look at the effeminate private.

"What the hell are you talking about?" Conner asked.

"Hitler's into the occult. I read about that in Life magazine before I got shipped over," Duff said. "He's trying all kinds of crap, trying to find historical relics and make new weapons, trying magic and voodoo and all kinds of crazy stuff. He's desperate to get an edge on us because he knows he's losing the war."

"So now he's bringing the dead back to life?" Kern asked.

"Not just any dead. Dead German soldiers," Duff said. "I heard that guy say '*Welcome back to the war, Major.*' Welcome *back*. They are bringing dead soldiers back to keep on fighting." Duff paused. "This could be Hitler's ultimate secret weapon. Unlimited soldiers."

"Get down!" Conner hissed.

They followed Conner's lead and crouched down even lower behind the brush.

Two of the German soldiers emerged from around the side of the building, leading two horses drawing a wooden cage behind them. The soldiers stopped as they reached the gravesite. They moved to the corpses laying in the snow and began shoving them one by one into the wooden cage. They jammed the dead bodies into the small area of the cage, pushing and shoving on them, kicking at them with their boots, until all the corpses were stuffed inside the wagon. Then the two Germans led the horses deeper into the cemetery.

The GIs followed the German soldiers, staying outside the cemetery perimeter, trying to follow the two Germans as best they could, but the two soldiers moved deeper into the cemetery and they lost them.

"Score, with me," Conner said. "Let's go see what they are doing." Scorelli nodded without a word. Conner glanced at the others. "Everybody else stay put."

Conner and Scorelli hid behind a large granite tombstone, each man peering out from one side of the huge block of stone. Their breaths whispered out of their mouths in faint plumes of misty white. A thin layer of fog swirled around their boots and legs.

Conner watched as the two German soldiers dragged a body out of the wagon cage and unceremoniously dumped the dead man into a massive pit dug in the ground. The soldiers methodically continued to add corpses to the pit. The huge hole in the earth had enough room for dozens more bodies, if not hundreds. The German soldiers finished unloading the bodies and moved away with the wagon. The two Americans stayed hidden as the wagon vanished back into the fog, neither one quite sure what their next move should be.

"Sarge," Scorelli whispered.

Conner looked over to the Italian to see Scorelli pointing off to his left. Conner followed his indicating finger and saw what Scorelli was looking at. There were at least a dozen shallow graves dug in the ground, momentarily visible as the fog shifted around them. All of them were similar to the grave where they had seen the naked man rise up out of the ground.

"Does that mean they are getting ready to bring back more of them?" Scorelli asked.

"Yes, it does," a voice said from behind them.

Conner whirled to see a German Hauptmann pointing a Luger at his chest. It was Hauptmann Frankel. And then Frankel fired, hitting Conner square in the chest with three deadly bullets.

"No!" Scorelli shouted.

Frankel quickly moved his aim to the young Italian private and fired. But the German missed.

Scorelli ducked, losing his grip on his rifle as he rolled towards the firing German soldier; the bullet careened off the granite tombstone, taking away a chunk of stone, sending bits of rock exploding in all directions. Scorelli drew his bayonet from his boot and slashed at Frankel's leg. The long knife was quicker for Scorelli to grab than the Colt shoved awkwardly into his belt. The sharp blade sliced through the German's pant leg and cut deep into flesh. The German howled and stooped to grab at his leg. Scorelli slashed him across his throat. Frankel dropped to the ground, gurgling and clutching at his sliced neck. Scorelli stabbed him several times in the chest to make certain the German was dead.

Scorelli quickly moved to Conner, but he knew the Sarge was dead from the glassy-eyed stare that looked back at him. He quickly glanced around the area. Scorelli feared the gunfire might bring more German soldiers, so he knew he couldn't linger. Tombstones of all shapes and sizes dotted the snow-covered land around him. Too much open terrain that way. He saw a small building nearby, its squat shape drifting in and out of his vision as the fog swirled around it. He snatched up his dropped rifle, and moved towards the structure, keeping low.

Scorelli reached the building and pressed his back flat against the brick wall. He struggled to calm his wild breathing, the bloody bayonet knife still clutched tightly in one hand, his rifle clutched in the other.

A soft moaning sound from inside the building drew his attention. There was a small window on the wall a few feet away from him. He eased slowly along the wall, moving towards the window. Scorelli cautiously peered inside the building and his eyes went wide.

"Do you like him?" Dr. Melange asked.

Helena was naked, sitting astride the Major, moving up and down over his hard shaft. "Oh, yes," she panted.

Dr. Melange watched with complete fascination. He moved closer to Helena, watching her pump her body up and down on the Major's cock. He turned to look at the Major. Dr. Melange could see something behind the resurrected man's eyes. He wasn't quite sure what it was, but there was something there. Was it the Major returned from the beyond, or was it something else? He wasn't sure. "Do you like her, Major?" the doctor asked the undead soldier.

The Major was quiet and still for a long moment. Then he reached up and grabbed Helena's shoulders. Dr. Melange could see the fear rise up in Helena's face. The Major held on to her tightly, then rose up, turning her over onto her back on the marble slab. He pulled her closer to the edge of the slab so he could penetrate her fully. He pounded himself into her. Helena took him deep, her breath turning wild and heated. She orgasmed again and again and again. Finally, she had enough. "Tell him to stop," she said, her words coming out in panting gasps.

"Major, you can stop now," Dr. Melange said.

The Major gave a few more aggravated thrusts and then pulled out of Helena. His thickness glistened with the residue of Helena's lust.

"What's wrong with him?" Helena asked. She eased herself to a sitting position on the marble slab.

Dr. Melange shook his head. "I don't know. Perhaps he cannot finish," the doctor said.

Helena squinted and frowned at him. "What?"

The doctor pointed to the Major's large erection. "He can't finish. Perhaps he has no fluids left."

Helena stared at the Major's glistening erection. "Doesn't he need blood to make that happen?" she asked.

"Perhaps it was in such a state when he died. I do not know. Raising the dead is a new skill for me. I do not have all the answers yet."

Helena continued to stare at the resurrected soldier's stiff member. "Is it going to stay like that?"

Dr. Melange shook his head. "I don't know. It might."

A soft crunching sound made Scorelli turn away from the window.

Two German soldiers moved slowly through the graveyard, their Sturmgewehr 44s held at the ready at their hips. The fog swirled around them, revealing an arm here and a leg there as they moved.

Scorelli raised his rifle and took careful aim, timing his shots, waiting until both of the soldiers were not obstructed by a tombstone or granite cross. He fired two well-placed bullets and both German soldiers went down. One of them continued to squirm on the ground so Scorelli put a final bullet into his chest.

Scorelli chanced a quick glance back into the room, but it was empty now. The blonde woman and the men were gone. Scorelli had seen enough. He needed to get back to the group. He moved cautiously through the graveyard, racing warily from one tombstone to the next, circling back around to where Conner had told the others to stay.

Kern wiped away angry tears from his dirty cheeks after Scorelli finished telling them what happened.

Sarge was dead. Sarge was dead! The reality of their situation hit him hard. They were just a bunch of scared kids without him. "We need the Sarge," Kern moaned. "Now what the hell are we going to do?"

"We keep fighting," Palinski said. "Right? That's what Sarge would want us to do, isn't it?"

Scorelli nodded. Duff hesitated, but then gave a quick nod.

"And the first thing we do is put those undead fucks back in the ground where they belong," Scorelli told them. "Let's go."

Kern didn't move to follow them. He wiped away more tears from his face.

Scorelli turned an angry stare back to Kern. "You comin', cry baby?"

Dr. Melange surveyed the room. His breath came out in thick white plumes as he moved inside the large refrigerated chamber that held hundreds of dead German soldiers. They were stacked like cordwood, five bodies high. They had ten newly resurrected soldiers now, ten of the zweite gelegenheit brigade, but he knew the Reich needed so much more. They needed thousands more, tens of thousands more, to defeat the fast approaching American and British troops.

"You guys ready?" Scorelli asked.

The others all nodded as they gripped their weapons, clutching them to their chests. Kern was with them, his face muddy with dried tears. They were pressed up against the wall of the building where Scorelli had earlier watched the blonde woman getting fucked by the undead German Major.

"I don't know how many are in there," Scorelli warned his fellow GIs. "Just be ready for anything."

The others nodded, their nervousness clearly rising. Kern struggled to still his trembling fingers.

Scorelli took a deep breath, then stepped around the corner of the building, bringing his rifle to bear in front of him.

No one was there.

They moved slowly, cautiously, into the building.

The first room they encountered was set up as a small communication station, with an array of radio equipment positioned on several desks in the corner of the room.

Kern moved towards the radio equipment, studying the equipment for a moment. "Maybe we can get a message out."

"Duff, you know how to work this thing?" Scorelli asked.

Duff moved over to the group, clutching a piece of paper in his hand he had just picked up off a nearby desk. "We've got a bigger problem." Duff held up the communique he was holding.

Scorelli looked over to him. "A bigger problem? How the fuck can we have a bigger problem than the Nazis raising dead German soldiers back to life?" Scorelli asked.

Duff waved the communique. "This says a wagon load of POWs is being brought in and two squads are coming in with it."

"Jesus," Kern said. "I wish the Sarge was still here. He would know what to do."

"Well, he ain't fucking here," Scorelli said. "We need to deal with it."

"Guys," Palinski called out in a hushed voice.

They all turned to look at Palinski who was staring through a small glass window of a nearby door.

"You need to come see this," Palinski said.

Scorelli opened the door to reveal a barracks. The walls were lined with bunk beds, two layers tall. Each bunk was comprised of a simple thin piece of wood for a bed; there were no blankets, no pillows, just a flat piece of wood. There were more than a hundred bunks in the room. Nine of them were occupied by the naked men they had seen around the gravesite earlier. The naked men all lay prone on separate bunks, their eyes open, their bodies deathly still. One of them had his head turned towards the door, his eyes open and staring.

The GIs stood motionless in the doorway, waiting for the things on the bunks to attack. But they didn't move.

"What the hell are they doing?" Palinski asked, his voice barely an audible whisper.

Kern motioned to the one German looking right at them. "Look at that one. He's looking right this way. Jesus, he's gotta see us."

"How come they're not moving?" Scorelli whispered.

They were all quiet for a long moment.

"They are being the perfect soldiers," Duff finally muttered. The others looked at Duff. Duff looked at the undead men on the bunks. "They are awaiting orders."

"How do we kill them?" Scorelli asked in a hushed tone. He took a few steps deeper into the barracks. The others stayed right behind him, following his lead. Scorelli glanced back at Duff, waiting for the answer.

Duff shook his head.

Scorelli frowned. "They didn't tell you how in all those Life magazine articles you read?" he asked.

Duff shook his head. "No. But that would have been pretty ironic, right? Life explaining how to kill the undead."

"Yeah, really fucking ironic," Scorelli said.

"What do we do with them?" Palinski asked.

Scorelli stared at the undead German soldiers, no answer coming from his lips.

"Cut off their heads," Kern said.

They all looked at Kern.

Kern shrugged. "Even if they are undead, I still think they need their heads to function."

They all stared quietly for a moment.

"Okay, who's gonna do it?" Scorelli asked.

"Fuck, I'll do it," Palinski said. "They are creeping the shit out of me." He drew his Fairbairn–Sykes fighting knife, a double-edged fighting knife resembling a dagger with a foil grip, and moved toward the motionless body closest to him.

"Shit, Palinski," Duff said. "What the hell are you going to do with that? Poke holes in his head?" He pushed Palinski aside and drew his M3 trench knife. The M3 had a thicker, meatier blade than the Fairbairn-Sykes knife. The others looked at Duff, surprised by his sudden macho aggressiveness, but said nothing. Duff eased forward and crouched down over the nearest dead German. The undead man's dull blue eyes stared at Duff, not blinking, not moving to follow Duff's actions. Duff slowly moved the tip of his knife towards the undead German's neck.

"Just cut him, man," Scorelli said. He glanced nervously at the door of the barracks, then back to Duff.

Duff touched the tip of his knife to the German's throat, getting ready to cut him, getting ready to sever his head from his body.

The undead German reacted sharply, grabbing at Duff's hand, gripping him tightly around his wrist. Duff shouted in alarm, unsuccessfully trying to yank his hand free of the undead soldier's fierce grip. The undead soldier grabbed Duff around the neck with his other hand and squeezed his throat, crushing Duff's windpipe with a sickening crunch. Duff's body went limp in the undead soldier's hand, the American's head flopping lifelessly to the side.

Scorelli fired point-blank into the undead German's head and its skull exploded in a torrent of shriveled grey brain matter and shards of bone.

A piece of skull bone hit another undead German soldier nearby and the Nazi creature rose up from its prone position, immediately moving to attack Scorelli. Scorelli reacted quickly, hitting the undead soldier in the upper chest and then blowing its head off with a second shot. *Ping.* The sound of his Garand ejecting its clip rang out. "I'm out!" Scorelli shouted as he quickly fumbled for a fresh clip.

Kern moved methodically up the left side row of bunks, blowing the heads off every undead soldier with his submachine gun as he moved past them.

Palinski mirrored his movement up the right row of bunks, firing his M1 point blank into the head of each undead German soldier.

It was over very quickly. Bits of brain and bone littered the bunks and the floors. Very little blood had come from the undead soldiers, but shreds of flesh stuck to the walls in dozens of places.

The room became very quiet.

The sound coming from the direction of the open doorway behind them froze all three men for a moment. Scorelli was the first to turn around. He stared at the man who used to be Major Helmut Schossenfiel standing naked in the doorway, his large erect penis making his shadowy visage somehow even more obscene and grotesque. Several knives were stuck in his body, as if he were using his undead flesh as a distorted sheath for the blades.

Behind the Major, Scorelli saw two other German soldiers, Dr. Melange, and the blonde woman Helena. One of the German soldiers raised his StG44, but the doctor put one of his black gloved hands on the weapon and pushed the gun barrel down. Dr. Melange took a step forward and closed the door behind the Major, locking the undead German commander in the barracks with the American soldiers. Scorelli could see Dr. Melange staring through the small glass window, an obvious eagerness still clearly visible in what little he could see of the doctor's face.

Scorelli raised his Garand and fired, but the undead Major moved quickly, ducking low and diving forward, his momentum bringing him right up to Scorelli. The Major grabbed the barrel of the gun and ripped it out of Scorelli's hands. The little Italian froze for just a moment, but that gave the Major enough time to drive his fist into Scorelli's chest, knocking the wind out of the GI. Scorelli gasped, doubling over as he clutched at his chest.

Palinski and Kern swung their weapons around to aim at the Major, but Scorelli was in their direct lines of fire. Palinski raced forward, lurching to the side, trying to maneuver into a position that would give him a clean shot at the Major.

The Major grabbed Scorelli by the arm and swung him at Palinski as if he were tossing a rag doll aside. Scorelli slammed into Palinski, sending them both tumbling into a bunk occupied by a brain-splattered undead German soldier.

Kern saw that he had a clean shot at the Major, so he took it, sending a dozen rounds into the Major's stomach and chest. The force of the bullets staggered the Major, but he quickly recovered. Kern had been aiming for his head, but his aim from his waist where he clutched the Thompson was way off. The Major drew a knife from his waist and hurled it with amazing speed and power. His aim was true. The blade penetrated Kern's thick jacket and sunk into his upper left shoulder.

Kern howled in pain, jerking back to his left as the knife penetrated his flesh. Bullets sprayed past the Major, moving up the barracks wall and into the ceiling as Kern's finger pulled tight on the trigger.

Scorelli and Palinski worked to untangle themselves, pushing the naked headless corpse away from them.

Scorelli scanned the area around him for his weapon. He saw his M1 on the ground in the middle of the barracks; he had lost his grip on the weapon when the Major had tossed him. Scorelli glanced down at his belt and saw that his Colt was gone, too, the gun somehow dislodged in the tussle.

Palinski brought his Garand up and fired at the approaching undead soldier. The bullet hit the Major in his upper right chest at the same time the *ping* of an empty Garand clip sounded. "Shit," Palinski said. "I'm out." He fumbled for a fresh clip, but his hand could not locate one on his belt. He glanced down at his waist and saw where the fresh clip was located. He grabbed at it, but fumbled it and dropped the clip to the barracks floor. He bent down to scoop up the clip, and then glanced up to see the Major not more than two feet away from him.

The Major gripped Palinski's head with both hands and rammed his stiff cock straight into Palinski's open, startled mouth. The force of the Major's thrust drove his rock-hard cock straight through the back of Palinski's neck. Blood sprayed outward from Palinski's neck as the bulbous cock head of the Major erupted out of the Pole's flesh like a snake erupting violently out of its burrow. Palinski's mouth stayed open in death as the Major withdrew his blood-stained cock from between the dead GI's lips.

Kern stared in wide-eyed terror as Palinski slumped lifelessly to the floor.

The Major closed in on Kern. The undead German's face was flat and expressionless. Kern could see no hatred, no malice, no anger. Just an emotionless indifference. The German soldier was a true killing machine now.

The Major reached Kern and ripped the knife out of Kern's shoulder. Blood sprayed upward into the Major's undead face as he jerked the blade out of

Kern's flesh. The Major raised the knife and then suddenly his face disintegrated, shredding into bone and brain and cold flesh. His body fell to the side and Kern saw Scorelli standing in the distance, his M1 raised to his face. Scorelli lowered his weapon, breathing hard.

"Get down!" Kern shouted at Scorelli as he saw the barracks door behind the little Italian opening.

Scorelli dove to the side, hitting the floor behind one of the bunks that contained a head-shredded German corpse. The Italian private smiled a grim smile as he saw his Colt M1911 laying on the floor within reach.

Kern fired, killing one of the German soldiers as the man tried to enter the room. Then Kern's gun was out of ammo. He froze for just a moment, then dove to the floor behind another bunk just as a spray of gunfire shredded the air where he had been standing just seconds before.

Scorelli grabbed his Colt from the floor and fired four quick blind shots at the German, just raising the pistol over the bunk and pulling the trigger. He hit the German twice, one bullet smashing into the soldier's right thigh, the other hitting the enemy combatant in the stomach. The German doubled over, stumbling, falling onto his right knee. Scorelli could see him from underneath the bunk. He aimed the Colt at the German's head and fired. The soldier didn't make a sound when the bullet penetrated his face; he just fell over and stopped moving.

The barracks became quiet for a long moment. From his vantage point behind the bunk, Scorelli could see the German doctor standing just beyond the doorway. The man looked frozen in shock.

Behind Dr. Melange, Scorelli caught a glimpse of blonde hair and knew the woman was just outside the room as well. He quickly moved to his feet and headed for the barracks door. "Kern, on me," he said. He didn't even bother to look to see if Kern followed him; he just assumed he would.

Kern followed him, loading a fresh clip into his Thompson as he scrambled after Scorelli, making sure his weapon was ready to fire again.

Both of the GIs moved into the room just outside the barracks, Scorelli with his M1911 at the ready, Kern with his submachine gun poised to fire from his waist.

Dr. Melange and Helena didn't move as the GIs entered the outer room. The two Germans both just seemed paralyzed with either shock or disbelief, or a combination of both.

"You speak English?" Scorelli asked.

Neither one of them answered.

Scorelli put his Colt right up against the doctor's forehead, pressing the barrel into his flesh. "You speak English?" he asked again.

"Ja... yes," Dr. Melange muttered.

"You mind telling me what you are doing here?" Scorelli asked, the feigned politeness in his words doing nothing to mask the rage in his tone.

"Apparently still losing the war," the doctor said with clear bitterness in his voice.

"Damn fucking straight you are still losing," Scorelli said. He pushed the barrel of his pistol even harder against the doctor's forehead. "What the fuck are you doing with all these dead bodies? I mean besides that slut fucking all of them."

"I am not a slut," Helena said.

"I saw you riding a Nazi zombie's cock," Scorelli said to her. "In my book, that makes you a slut."

"You saw what?" Kern asked. He looked at Helena, then back to Scorelli.

"Never mind," Scorelli told him.

Helena moved and Scorelli fired towards her, just missing her; bullets chewed into the wall behind her and the wall spit back splinters of wood that landed all around her booted feet. "Don't move," Scorelli ordered her.

Helena remained still.

Scorelli poked the end of the M1911 pistol back against Dr. Melange's head, making no attempt to be gentle. "I'm still waiting for an answer."

"You know very well what we are doing," the doctor replied, wincing.

"How? How is that possible?" Scorelli asked.

"How indeed. Such knowledge holds great power."

Scorelli tightened his expression, his lips going taut. His finger started to curl with greater force on the Colt's trigger.

"You kill me and you'll never get the answer." The doctor's face was grim and his cold eyes held a strange confidence.

Scorelli pulled the trigger. *Click.* The Colt was out of ammo.

"No!" Kern pushed Scorelli's gun down. "We need him alive."

Beads of sweat immediately formed on the doctor's forehead. The confidence disappeared from his eyes.

"Why the hell do we need this sick fuck alive?" Scorelli asked as he inserted a bullet into the Colt and reached for another round.

"Because we need him to bring the Sarge back."

Scorelli looked up from re-loading his pistol and frowned at Kern. "Are you out of your mind?"

"You heard what Duff said. There's a couple of German squads headed our way. We need the Sarge. He'll know what to do."

"He's dead, Leo. I saw him die."

Kern shook his head. "We can bring him back." He pointed to Dr. Melange. "He can bring him back."

"No, he can't," Scorelli said.

"Why not?"

"Because he's dead." Scorelli raised his reloaded pistol and fired, putting a bullet into Dr. Melange's forehead.

Bits of bone and brain and blood splattered all over Helena's white parka, staining it with a spray of deep crimson blotches. She startled, throwing her hands up to shield her face but moving too late to block the blood from splashing all over her cheeks and into her mouth.

Scorelli watched the German doctor fall lifelessly to the floor. "I don't need the answer. I hope it dies with you."

"Damn it, Score, what did you do that for?"

Scorelli looked over to Kern.

Kern's head drooped with disappointment. "We could have brought the Sarge back to fight with us."

Scorelli frowned at Kern.

"Why not?" Kern asked. "We could've used these fuckers' sick power against them."

Scorelli's frown deepened. "You really would want to raise the Sarge from the dead?" Scorelli shook his head. "That ain't right. The Sarge paid his dues."

"So we just leave him dead in some Nazi cemetery?" It was Kern's turn to shake his head. "I don't think he would have wanted that, I really don't."

"Are you crazy?"

"I think he would've wanted to keep fighting. No matter what."

Scorelli was quiet for a moment. "Well, it's too late now. I hope that secret died with him." Scorelli motioned with his pistol to the dead German doctor at his feet. "Nobody should have that knowledge."

"Maybe she knows how to do it," Kern said, looking at Scorelli then at Helena. He stared hard at the blonde German woman. "You know how all this works? You know how to bring them back?"

"She don't know. She's just a stupid German bitch."

"Oh, she knows," Kern said.

"She does, huh? How do you figure that?"

"I can see it in her eyes."

"What, she got the secret etched into her pupils somewhere? She reflecting the magic potion formula back out of her fucking eye sockets?" Scorelli frowned. "How the fuck can you see it in her eyes? Let's just waste her and get out of here. We ain't draggin' no German bitch through the forest with us."

Kern looked calmly at Helena. "You have about one minute to tell us the truth or you will die. You understand that?"

"Yes, I understand," she said in English. Her voice had just a hint of a guttural German accent, but the words were very clear.

"Do you know how to bring the dead back to

life?"

"Yes."

The easy quickness of her answer gave Kern pause. He looked at Scorelli, failed miserably at giving him a triumphant smirk, then looked back to Helena. "Show us how."

She shook her head.

Scorelli shook his head. "This all just wrong, Leo. You need to let it go."

"There's a truckload of prisoners headed this way and two squads of German soldiers. You think just the two of us can stop them?"

"You think bringing the Sarge back is going to stop them?"

"And Duff and Palinski. We can bring all three of them back," Kern said.

"Listen to what you are saying, Leo. You want to bring dead men back to life. You want to bring our friends back to life. They are dead. They should stay dead."

"If you knew the position we were in, would you want to come back?"

Scorelli frowned.

"I would," Kern said. "If I knew you guys were in trouble, I would want you to bring me back. I would."

Scorelli shook his head.

"You telling me, you wouldn't?" Kern asked.

Scorelli was quiet for a moment. Then he waved his pistol at Helena. "She ain't gonna help us, anyway."

"Oh, she'll help us," Kern said.

"She will?"

Kern nodded. "She will." He drew his bayonet. "Or I will skin her alive."

"Okay," Scorelli said with casual acceptance of the ugly threat. "But before you do that, I think we oughta have a little fun with her, don't you?"

Kern looked questioningly at Scorelli.

"She likes cock. We might as well give her some."

Kern frowned. "Are you kidding me? You want to rape her?" He glowered at Scorelli for a moment. "I always had a feeling you were a greasy pig, now I know for sure."

"Fuck you, Kern. We ain't gonna live to see the sunrise so why not have a little fun before we go." Scorelli looked at Helena. "Besides, you should have seen her riding that dead German cock. She was having the time of her fucking life. I could see it in her face, man. And if she enjoys dead German cock, just think how much she's gonna enjoy some live Italian cock." Scorelli winked at Helena. "Ain't that right, honey?"

"Damn it, Score. Keep it in your pants," Kern said, scowling. "Where's the Sarge? Where's his body?"

Helena crossed her arms over her chest, a hint of fear crossing her features. She looked at Kern. "I will help you bring your men back." She paused to look at Scorelli, then back to Kern. "But you need to keep him away from me."

Scorelli raised his weapon and pointed it straight at her face. "You don't tell us what to fucking do, you stupid bitch. You got that?"

Helena remained calm in the face of Scorelli's ire. She looked at Kern. "The longer we wait, the more difficult it is to bring them back."

Kern looked questioningly at Helena. "So what do we need to do?"

"Now we need blood," the German woman replied. "The fresh blood of a man."

Kern motioned to one of the dead German soldiers on the barracks floor. "What about his?"

Helena shook her head. "It's been too long. We need very fresh blood."

Scorelli shook his head at her. "The only thing that's been too long is my dick without pussy." He looked at Helena. "Time to get busy, fraulein." He reached for his belt.

Kern stared a hard cold stare at Scorelli.

<hr />

Private Leo Kern wondered if he had made the right decision. Sacrifices had to be made in war, didn't they? They had to always give themselves the best chance to defeat the enemy, no matter what. Isn't that what Sarge taught them? The Sarge was the best soldier in their group by far. He had killed more Germans than all of them combined.

Kern looked at Sergeant Thomas Conner for a long moment. The Sarge had no more need for food, no need for sleep, no need for shelter. He had but one purpose now for all eternity: to fulfill his duty as a soldier and kill as many of the enemy as he could. Kern knew he hadn't saved Sarge's life, but giving the Sarge a second chance to keep fighting was just as good, wasn't it? "You ready to kill some more Nazis, Sarge?"

Conner didn't answer. He gripped the Thompson submachine gun in his pale hands. Kern thought he saw a hint of a grim smile turn up the corners of Sarge's lips, but when he looked closer the steely smirk was gone.

Kern gripped his weapon and stared up the snow-covered road leading into the cemetery, ignoring the pain in his shoulder where the undead Major had knifed him. He could probably bring back Duff and Palinski, too. Hell, now that the German woman had shown him the secret maybe he would even bring back Scorelli.

He just needed more fresh blood.

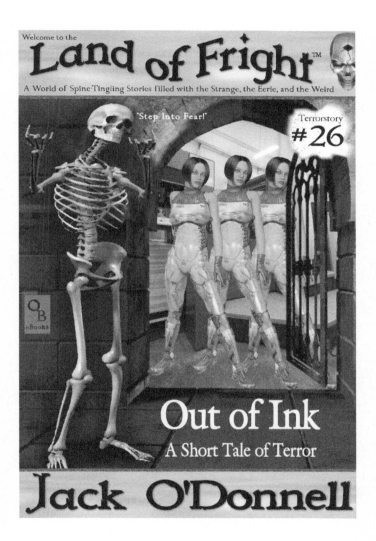

Welcome to the

Land of Fright™

A World of Spine-Tingling Stories filled with the Strange, the Eerie, and the Weird

"Step Into Fear!"

Terrorstory
#26

OB eBooks

Out of Ink

A Short Tale of Terror

Jack O'Donnell

TERRORSTORY #26
OUT OF INK

"It's out of ink."

"What the hell do you mean it's out of ink?"

"It's out of ink means it's out of ink."

Tyrell Rikort frowned a deep frown. "Don't we have spare ink in storage?" Tyrell was a tall man with dark brown skin and a head devoid of any hair. He had a long, narrow face and a large forehead. His deep hazelnut eyes were very troubled. He was dressed in his corporate blue jumpsuit; the uniform was a soft shade of blue, a tight-fighting one-piece with the Morloi Mining Company logo emblazoned on the left breast.

Frendel Alamin shook his head. "No. We've got more coming in the next shipment, but it won't be here for months." Frendel had pale pink skin, a soft rounded chin, and pale blue eyes. He had a small patch of black hair topping his head. He was shorter than Tyrell, and his corporate jumpsuit was much wider in the waist.

They stood in front of the bioprinter, lamenting the red flashing light that silently announced the dearth of necessary supplies to make the printer function as needed. The machine took up most of the room, with an elaborate array of nozzles and tubing situated along its length. An empty platform filled the middle of the machine where the final product was produced.

Tyrell stared at the empty platform. "How the hell did this happen?"

"The new epidermal layer takes extra time and uses extra ink. We've already gone through the two units of spares we had in storage."

"We need to print more warriors, God damn it." Tyrell grit his teeth. "The Eskelon are basically at our damn doors."

Frendel frowned at him. "You think I don't know that?"

Tyrell was quiet for a moment. "*We'll* have to fight them."

Frendel looked at him as if he were mad.

"What other choice do we have?" Tyrell asked.

"Do you even know how to fire that blaster?" Frendel glanced down at the weapon holstered at Tyrell's side. "I've never even seen you hold the thing, let alone try to shoot something with it."

Tyrell put his hand on the black metal grip of his blaster, but left the weapon safely secured in its holster. "Don't you just aim and shoot?"

"They've got thick shells. You'll need to aim and shoot with incredible precision if you want to take an Eskelon down."

"The warriors can do it pretty easily," Tyrell said. "I've seen them take an Eskelon down with two or three shots. Sometimes even one head shot."

"It's not a head shot. It's a neck shot. Their heads are fully armored and their skulls are dense enough to deflect a blaster strike with minimal damage done."

Tyrell waved his hand. "Whatever."

Frendel continued. "And they can take an Eskelon down in one shot because the warriors are programmed to do so. The most up to date schematics of the Eskelon biology are downloaded into the program before we print them out."

"So you don't think we can hold them back?"

"We're not fighters. We're bureaucrats," Frendel said. "Look, the warriors have skin density triple what ours is. Their bone structure is twice as strong. Their reflex speed is at least double ours, if not quadruple. They can fight the Eskelons far better than we'll ever be able to. That's why we print them. Without them…" Frendel just let his voice trail off.

"So we can't even last a few months until the next shipment of ink comes in." It came out as more of a statement than a question from Tyrell's lips.

Frendel shook his head. "Not without the warriors. Not against the intensity of the Eskelon's new attacks. The Eskelon are determined as hell to get us. And it doesn't look like they are slowing down the pace of their attacks. If anything, they are getting more frequent." Frendel pointed to a nearby monitor.

They watched another Eskelon attack being displayed on the big monitor near the bioprinter. The

Eskelons were quadruped creatures with spindly legs and a hard exoskeleton. They reminded Tyrell of the big cockroaches he had seen on DeLora, but the Eskelons had fewer legs and no antennae. And the Eskelons were far bigger. Most of them were about three to four feet long, but they had seen some recently as long as six feet and as wide as three feet. They had a dull brown color to them, very similar to the soil color near Mine 7. Their exoskeleton coloring was one of the reasons why they hadn't noticed them at first when they chose the spot for Mine 7. The Eskelon camouflage patterns were excellent, mimicking the soil and rock patterns in the area, thus keeping them hidden from view from the patrols that had been done near Mine 7.

The Eskelon were now massed in the north quadrant. They repeatedly attacked the fence that surrounded the Morloi Mining facility, charging at the barrier in wave after wave. The fence was an energy barrier twenty feet high, the walls of the fence glowing and crackling with a blue energy. Thick posts broke up the fence about every fifty yards. Each post generated a beam that created the blue energy barrier wall between each metal upright. The energy fence was the only thing holding the Eskelon horde back.

That and the warriors waging battle against them. The warriors were humanoid in appearance, but they had a sturdier look to them, a thicker look to their skin. They moved with amazing speed and agility, assessing the vector of the Eskelon attacks and mounting quick defensive strikes with well-aimed blaster blasts and expertly thrown energy grenades from their positions atop the posts.

Tyrell and Frendel continued to watch the activity

playing out on the monitor. Several warriors held their ground just outside the fence, firing as quickly as they could at the attacking horde. Dozens of Eskelon squealed and dropped dead to the ground. But for each Eskelon that fell, it looked like a dozen more Eskelon took its place. The level of attacks did appear to be intensifying.

One of the Eskelon reached the fence barrier and hooked its claw into one of the metal posts that generated the energy beams. A warrior shot the attacking creature in the exposed part of its neck and the Eskelon's head exploded off its body in a torrent of their yellow blood and dark green brain matter. Another Eskelon charged straight into the electrified wall and was immediately fried by the strong current. A warrior's well-aimed blast took out another charging Eskelon, then another. Several more Eskelons hit the energy barrier and immediately crackled under the intense energy, dying instantly. The pile of Eskelon bodies lying dead along the energy fence grew. Yet they kept coming.

Another Eskelon piggybacked off the newly dead pile of its fellow Eskelons, climbing atop their corpses near the energy barrier, then leaped up and over the electrified wall. It landed inside the security perimeter and glanced around, hissing as it surveyed its surroundings. A warrior inside the fence raced over to the invading Eskelon and shot it in the leg, maiming it. The Eskelon screeched and the warrior finished it off with two point blank blaster blasts to its neck, severing its head from its body.

"It breached the fence." Tyrell turned to Frendel. "It breached the fence." His face was etched with incredulous disbelief. And the beginnings of real fear.

Frendel nodded. "It's the third time I've seen it."

"The third time?"

Frendel said nothing. The warriors were doing a valiant job keeping the attacking Eskelons at bay, but he knew they would soon be overwhelmed without reinforcements. The time to act was now.

Tyrell looked at Frendel. "We can't wait."

Frendel nodded.

⋘⋘❈⋙⋙

The newly arrived colonists gathered in the common room. It was a huge room that served as a dining area and a community meeting room. Dozens and dozens of tables were arranged in rows throughout the room, each table large enough to seat ten. A gigantic screen filled one wall; this is where corporate announcements were shown, and holo-movies on the weekends. Smaller screens were embedded in each table.

The colonists were all still dressed in their dull grey sleep suits, many of them still looking haggard and weary, shaking off the after effects of months of travel sleep. They sat in the formerly pristine white chairs before the formerly pristine white tables. Now all the chairs and the tables were marred with scratches and worn down with years of repeated use from the tens of thousands of miners who worked on the planet.

"Welcome to Mira Twelve." Tyrell stood before the group, dressed in his official welcoming uniform. This uniform was also a tight-fighting jumpsuit with the Morloi Mining Company logo emblazoned on the left breast, but it was a darker shade of blue than his casual uniform.

Frendel moved about the group, handing each one of them a glass half-filled with a clear liquid. He was also dressed in his formal dark blue Morloi uniform.

"Tell us about the Eskelons," someone in the crowd shouted.

Murmurings of assent spread through the gathered group as heads bobbed up and down.

"Tell us."

Tyrell stood calmly before them. "There is nothing for you to worry about. You just need to worry about fulfilling your responsibilities. Each of you has a purpose." Tyrell studied the faces of the new arrivals. They were scattered amongst half a dozen tables. A dark-skinned man looked at him with curious eyes. He was the one who had shouted out the demand to tell them about the Eskelons. Another brown-skinned man studied the glass of liquid he had been given, sniffing at its contents. A blonde-haired woman sat close to him, her head hung low. She was having a bad time with the side effects of travel sleep. She probably had a helluva skull throb going on.

"Why are they attacking the colony?" the dark-skinned man with curious eyes asked.

More muttering spread through the group.

Tyrell held up his hand. "It was an accident. Our mining destroyed one of their caves before we even knew the Eskelon existed. We didn't know they were natives to this world. They have taken it as an attack and are retaliating."

"Can we communicate with them?" This question came from a dark-skinned woman to his right. She looked fit and well rested, clearly a veteran of travel sleep.

Tyrell shook his head. "We have tried, but they

don't respond to any electronic signals. We don't think they are even aware of that form of communication."

"Do they have a language?"

"Nothing that we can decipher."

"Are they just animals?"

Tyrell nodded. "That's what we think. We believe they are wild animals protecting their young and their territory."

"How can we mine the trontium if they keep attacking the operations?" the dark-skinned man asked. "I'm here for one reason and one reason only. To fill up my account with credits."

Heads nodded all around him.

"The warriors keep them at bay," Tyrell said.

This quieted the group, but only for a brief moment. Then the chattering and rumblings got even louder. Even the travel-sleep-weary woman raised her head to look at him with exhausted eyes.

"You have warriors here?" the dark-skinned woman asked.

"Aren't they outlawed?" someone else asked.

Tyrell shook his head. "Not out here."

More murmurings spread through the newly arrived colonists. The warriors had been banned from the Home Worlds decades ago, but they were still put to good use on the Outer Fringes. Mira Twelve was most definitely still considered a Fringe World, and probably always would be. It wasn't suitable for permanent habitation; it was perfect for mining colonies to extract trontium, a resource vital for interstellar travel, but that was about all the planet was good for. It was too harsh and too barren for much else.

Tyrell held up his hands, silencing the group for a moment. He pointed to one of the glasses that Frendel had handed out. The brown-skinned man had already drained it of its contents. "Please, everyone needs to drink." Tyrell looked at the travel-weary woman. Her glass was still untouched. "You will not be allowed out of this area until you do so. It contains vital antibodies and anti-viral properties that you all need to live on Mira Twelve."

The haggard-looking woman frowned, but she grabbed her glass and drank the liquid, emptying the glass. All of the other new arrivals followed suit.

⁂

Serak Fin woke up feeling very disoriented. The effects of the Nalarian flu still lingered in his body, but they were fading. He could feel it. The aches in his muscles were still there, and so was the stuffiness in his head, but he did feel better. The aches were less severe and he could actually breathe through one of his nostrils. He was a wiry man with a thin layer of blond hair covering his head. He had deep blue eyes and an easy smile when it came to his lips, but right now he felt no urge to smile.

He slowly sat up and swung his feet out of the sleep pod, placing them on the cold steel floor. He rubbed at his temples, slowly allowing himself to get his bearings. We must be on Mira Twelve, he thought. I don't hear the star engines humming or feel them vibrating. Despite the lingering discomfort of travel sleep and the healing aches from his body fighting off the Nalarian flu, Serak felt a sense of growing elation. He made it. He was finally on Mira Twelve. He now smiled his easy smile. Ready to start a new life. Finally

137

out of the grind of the desk job that was slowly killing him. Sure, the trontium mines were underground, but at least he'd be outside, not trapped inside a cubicle grinding out meaningless report after report for his corporate masters.

He donned his soft sole shoes and slowly got to his feet. He stood still for a moment, fighting back a wave of dizziness. Coming out of travel sleep was always a bit unsettling at first, especially moving to a standing position after being prone for so long. He headed out of the sick room towards the main sleep chamber. He entered the large room and glanced around at the sleep pods. The sleep pods were situated in five rows of ten. All of their lids were raised, their interiors empty. Everyone else was already up and about. It had been a full load this time. All fifty pods had been filled with eager passengers.

Serak glanced to the sleeping pod on the far left. Geenah wasn't there. His wife was already up. His wife was lucky he had taken ill right before the flight, otherwise she would have had to wait for the next flight. They had put him into one of the three sick pods the spacecraft was supplied with, allowing room for one more passenger to board. His wife had taken the pod that had been assigned to him. It was a violation of protocol, but an extra hundred note to one of the officials at the spaceport had eased the official's mental anguish for breaking the law.

Serak smiled at the thought of Geenah. He missed her and couldn't wait to see her smile back at him. He loved watching the corners of her eyes crinkle when she laughed. He felt like he hadn't seen his wife for years. It was one of those weird after effects of travel sleep. He thought it would be the exact opposite, that the months spent in travel sleep would seem like days, but they felt like years every time he came out of travel sleep. He was still a bit apprehensive about their move to Mira Twelve, but he was determined to make a new start. He wanted to be a better provider for his wife, and a better husband.

Serak glanced around the room at all the other sleep pods. How long have we been here? Probably not too long, he realized as he saw the luggage bags still sitting in piles near the door. They were probably at the welcoming ceremony, he realized. They haven't even come back yet to gather up their clothes. Maybe I can still make it.

<hr />

Tyrell pointed to a large view screen which displayed a group of warriors who were easily holding an attacking throng of Eskelons at bay. "See," he said to his two young sons standing at his side. "There's nothing to be afraid of. The warriors are doing their job."

"Those are new warriors, aren't they?" his eldest son asked as he intently studied the action happening on the view screen — a warrior outside the electronic fence sprinted over to a rock, braced her arm on the rock, and fired half a dozen shots with incredible precision. Three Eskelons dropped dead, all of them having their heads blown off right at the point where their necks were joined to their bodies. "I don't recognize any of them," his eldest son added.

Tyrell nodded. "Yes, they are. We just printed them out hours ago and they are already performing spectacularly."

Tyrell's wife, Iona, stood on the opposite side of

him from their sons. She was a petite woman with short brunette hair and a soft angled faced with just a hint of cheekbones showing. She grabbed Tyrell's hand and squeezed it. He squeezed her fingers reassuringly back.

Frendel stood next to Iona. He had no other family. Tyrell's family was the closest he ever came to having a family of his own. Tyrell's boys called him Uncle Frendel and he liked that, even though they weren't related at all.

"Hello?" A questioning voice and a shuffling sound coming from behind them made them turn.

❈❈❈❈❈

Serak stumbled into the common room. The large room was empty but for two men and a woman dressed in their casual corporate Morloi Mining Company attire. Two young boys were also with them, dressed in soft blue coveralls. They were all watching something on a view screen situated on the table in front of them. "Hello?" Serak said. "Where is everybody?" he asked.

The tall dark man started and whirled around to face him. The man stared hard at him. "Who the hell are you?"

"I'm Serak. I was in a sick pod. I caught a touch of Nalarian flu right before we left."

The woman smiled at Serak, but the two men glared at him with no attempt at masking their hostility.

"But I'm feeling better, thanks for asking." Serak looked around the room again. "Where is everybody from my ship?"

The tall dark man turned to the squat pale man. "I

thought we had all the colonists accounted for."

"That ship only holds fifty sleep pods," the pale man replied. "I counted fifty in the chamber."

Serak looked at them. "I told you. I was in one of the sick pods." He rubbed at his temples. "Why isn't anyone answering my question? Where is everybody? I want to see my wife."

And then Serak saw her. Not standing in the common room waiting for him as he had expected. Not running towards him with a big smile and open arms to embrace him. He saw Geenah's face on the view screen in front of him. Serak stepped up to the monitor and circled her face with his finger, enlarging the image. For a long moment, Serak just stared at the image of his wife's face. But it wasn't his wife's body. The body was bigger, thicker, and full of muscles. "What is going on? Why does that woman have my wife's face?" Serak looked over to the two men.

The pale man held a blaster aimed straight at Serak's chest.

"Uncle Frendel, what are you doing?" one of the young boys asked.

"Iona, take the boys," the tall dark man said.

Serak saw the woman frown.

"What is going on, Tyrell?" she asked. She clearly was confused by the events playing out.

The tall dark man's face grew severe. He never took his gaze away from Serak. "Iona, take the boys and go."

The woman put her arms around the boys' shoulders and herded them out of the room.

Serak stared straight at the man holding the blaster aimed at his chest. "You going to tell me what the hell is going on here?"

Serak watched a band of warriors beat back an attacking wave of Eskelon on the big view screen in front of him. Tyrell and Frendel stood behind him. Frendel still held the blaster, keeping it aimed at Serak as they watched him view the warriors repelling the Eskelons.

"We needed ink. We needed it for the warriors," Tyrell said.

Serak shook his head. His face was streaked with tears, his eyes laced with red jagged slashes of agony. "Ink?" His tone was incredulous. "You really tell yourself it's just ink? What did you do? Mince them up and toss them into the printer?" He fought back another wave of sobs.

They were still in the common room, but now it was empty except for the three of them. Tyrell and Frendel admitted what they had done to the newly arrived colonists and Serak had gone berserk, throwing chairs, flipping over tables. Frendel nearly shot him with the blaster, but Tyrell stayed his hand.

"Nothing as crude as that, no," Tyrell said. "They all — went quickly."

Serak snorted a bitter laugh. "They all *went quickly*? My wife *went quickly*? You trying to make yourself feel better? You murdered them! What are you? Some kind of monsters?"

Tyrell shook his head. "The Eskelon are the monsters. And if we don't hold them off, we'll all die. We couldn't wait for the next supply ship. We needed more warriors and we needed them now."

Serak scoffed. "A supply ship. Is that what you call it? What is it, full of old women and abandoned children?"

"Of course not," Frendel said, shaking his pale head. "It's full of convicted criminals that have been sentenced to death. At least they'll serve some purpose for the greater good." He looked over to Tyrell. "We don't need to explain ourselves to him. It was for the good of the colony." He aimed the blaster at Serak. "He can join his wife."

"No!" Tyrell shouted. He immediately lowered his voice. "No, Frendel. No more."

Serak said nothing. He stared hard and cold at them.

"Should we just let this colony die?" Frendel asked. "Are the lives of those fifty worth the lives of tens of thousands of colonists?"

Serak said nothing. He blinked away the tears that filmed his eyes. Geenah was gone. These monsters had killed her and fed her into the bioprinter. His knees buckled and he fell to the ground, putting his hands to his head. "Dear God, what have you monsters done?"

"A difficult choice had to be made and so we made it," Tyrell said.

Suddenly, Serak lunged at Tyrell, snatching the blaster out of his holster. He fired at Frendel, hitting him square in the chest. The energy blast crushed the squat man's chest, the force of the beam propelling him twenty feet in the air. Frendel's body hit a table and sent it tumbling to the ground as he crashed into it. Several chairs went flying in different directions.

Serak rose up and took several steps back away from Tyrell, leveling the weapon square at Tyrell's chest. "My choice won't be difficult at all."

Serak watched the bioprinter work. Each layer of flesh was laid in with extreme precision on top of the last, immediately joining seamlessly with the layer below it. A nozzle above the printer layered in the thick skeletal structure. Within minutes, half of the body was recognizable, the internal organs being printed from the top printer as the thick outer skin was laid down from the side printers. Moments later, the bioprinter made a soft ringing sound. Ding. A new warrior was born. A warrior born of recycled human flesh.

Serak stared at the warrior. It had a very strong resemblance to Tyrell, the former commander of the Mira Twelve colony. He would send this one to the front lines of the battle to join the one who looked like the pale man Frendel.

He turned to look at the two dozen freshly printed copies of his wife Geenah who waited for him. The warrior women all smiled at him and the corners of all their eyes crinkled. Serak smiled softly back at them. He would be a good husband and a good provider. To all of them.

Serak thought about the tens of thousands of colonists who populated Mira Twelve. If the colony needed more warriors to survive, he would give them more warriors. He wouldn't run out of ink for quite some time.

144

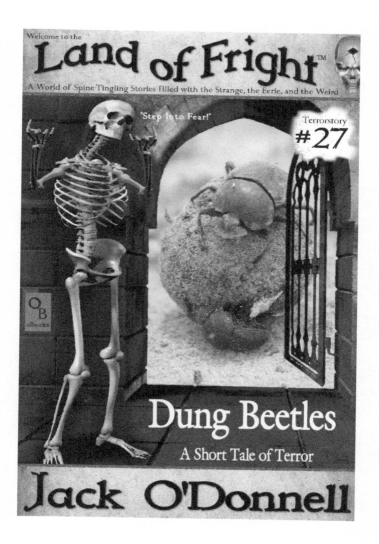

TERRORSTORY #27
DUNG BEETLES

"**I** gotta go," Billy said. "It's peekin' out."

"That's disgusting," Charlene said, frowning at her younger brother as she glanced over the front seat at him.

"I can't help it. I gotta go." Billy squirmed in the back seat. "I been holding it for hours."

"Yeah, well keep holding it. We're not stopping yet." Charlene turned back around to face the front. A sign blinking up on the right side of the road caught her gaze. "Look, it's flashing. Mom, it's flashing. What does that mean?"

Jean McDonall looked over to the road sign her daughter pointed at. Jean was in her mid-forties with short red hair. Middle aged plumpness had settled around her mid-section and the corners of her eyes were etched with permanent wrinkles. Raising four kids had taken its toll on her both mentally and physically. Her other two children were staying with their grandmother, so at least she didn't have to deal with four squabbling children. Just two. The three of them were driving in the remote hills of Pennsylvania, heading to New York to drop Charlene off at college; Billy had tagged along just for fun. Jean stared at the sign. *"Urgent Message When Flashing,"* the sign read. And it was indeed flashing. "Turn the radio to that channel." Jean pointed to the road sign. "It says AM 1610. Tune it to that."

Charlene fiddled with the presets on the radio, but none of them were set to 1610. She was eighteen, Jean's oldest child and the first one to go off to college. Charlene had a similar plumpness to her belly, very much the same body type as her mother. She wore thick-rimmed tortoise shell glasses. Her hair was also cut short, framing her cherubic face.

"You need to do it manually. Switch it to AM. Hurry up."

"Okay, okay. Jeez Louise." Charlene pushed the button on the radio to switch it to AM, then found 1610 after a moment of whipping through the numbers.

"Turn around!" the voice on the radio said. It was a loud, blaring voice, a voice filled with urgency. "If you are heading east on Highway 97 towards Arentown and you can hear this, stop your car immediately and turn around!"

Jean felt her fingers tighten on the wheel.

"What direction are we heading?" Billy asked from

his position in the back seat. Billy was fourteen, gangly, and awkward. His hair was long and wild, a mass of dark unruly curls. The beginnings of acne dotted his chin.

"East," Jean replied.

"Aren't we on Highway 97?" Billy asked.

No one answered.

"Turn around!" the voice on the radio said again. The voice sounded louder, the urgency even more heightened. "If you are heading east on 97 towards Arentown, turn around! If you want to live, turn around!" And then static spit out of the radio.

The Welcome to Arentown sign flashed by on their right.

"Did that sign just say *Welcome to Arentown?*" Billy asked.

"Did it?" Jean asked, a frown deepening her already wrinkled brow.

"Mom, stop the car," Billy said. "Didn't you hear what that guy said? Stop the car and turn around."

"We are *not* turning around," Charlene said, her voice firm. "I have to get to NYU." Charlene flipped the radio back to FM and a country music song filled the car.

"Oh," Billy said, his voice snide. "I guess you don't want to live then."

"Shut up, Billy," Charlene said.

"Holy crap! Are both of you deaf? That's what the radio said! Didn't you hear what the guy said? He said *Turn around if you want to live.*'"

Jean kept driving.

"Mom, you need to turn around," Billy said.

"No, keep going," Charlene countered.

Billy unhooked his seat belt and reached over into

the front seat from the back seat where he was sitting. He flipped the radio dial back to AM, trying to get the voice back. The sounds of talk radio stations flitted past as he twirled the dial.

"Billy, get back in your seat and put that seat belt back on," Jean said firmly.

"We need to find that station."

"Now, Billy. Don't make me pull over."

Billy sat back down in the backseat and crossed his arms over his chest. "I want you to pull over."

"Billy, put that seat belt on right now," Jean demanded.

Charlene turned around in her seat to glare at her brother, her seat belt tugging at her shoulders. "Billy, put your damn seat belt on."

"No."

Charlene turned to Jean. "Mom, make him put his seat belt on."

"Billy, so help me, if I have to pull this car over you are going to regret it."

Suddenly, the back window exploded in a rain of glass particles, showering Billy with shards of glass.

Jean screamed in alarm and swerved violently. The car went careening off the road, heading straight towards the sheer cliff wall that rose up a few dozen feet from the edge of the remote stretch of mountainous highway they were traveling on.

"Mom!" Charlene shrieked, pointing at the looming wall of stone.

Jean regained control of the car and swerved away from the rock wall, slamming on the brakes. Charlene's body thrust sharply forward, but her seat belt held her back, snapping tight against her shoulder and upper chest.

Billy slammed into the back of the front seat; he grunted as he bounced hard off of it. The force of the bounce pushed him back into the rear seat padding. His arms and legs flopped in haphazard directions as he lay sprawled across the back seat. "Something's in the car!" Billy cried out.

"What?" Jean asked. She shut the car off and fumbled at her seat belt, struggling to unlatch it.

"It's in my pants. It's crawling up my leg!" Billy smacked at his leg, fidgeting wildly, trying to get at whatever was moving up his leg. "It's crawling up me!"

"Charlene, help him!" Jean shouted as she continued to struggle with her seat belt.

Charlene unlatched her own seat belt and turned, leaning over the back seat to look at Billy.

Billy wildly smacked at his leg, fidgeting like mad as he fought at whatever was crawling up his leg. He tried to smack the back of his thigh, but couldn't reach it. "It's crawling up my leg!" There was true terror in Billy's voice now.

"Clench tight. Don't let it in."

"Clench what? Oh my God. It's there. I feel it! It's going in my—" And then Billy stopped talking. His eyes rolled into the back of his head.

"Billy!"

"What's wrong with him?" Charlene asked from the driver's seat, glancing at them through the rearview mirror. Jean sat in the backseat with Billy, his head cradled in her lap. Behind them, pieces of the shattered rear window lay sprinkled on the back window ledge. Air streamed in and swirled around them, ruffling Jean's hair.

"I don't know." Jean swiped away at the tears streaming down her face. "Just keep driving." She pointed to the Arentown exit that was fast approaching on their right. "Take that exit."

"That guy on the radio said to turn around. Maybe we shouldn't go to Arentown," Charlene said.

"I don't care. I have to get Billy to a doctor. This is the closest exit. Just get off here."

Charlene said nothing. She veered the car to the right, heading off the highway onto the Arentown exit ramp.

"He said it was crawling on him. What was crawling on him?" Charlene asked.

"I don't know!"

"Well, fucking look, Mom!"

Jean looked down at Billy. His head was cradled in her lap. His face was pale, his breathing shallow. She reached down and unbuckled his belt, yanking on it to tug it free of the loops on his jeans. She shifted in the seat, moving her body so Billy could lay flat on the backseat. She tugged at his jeans, pulling them down his legs. She exposed his underwear, then kept tugging the jeans down farther, exposing his legs.

"Do you see anything?" Charlene looked at her through the rearview mirror.

"No." Jean studied her son's legs. "Wait, yes. Some kind of scratches." There were tiny red marks running up his right leg.

"So something *was* crawling on him."

Jean followed the red scratches up Billy's leg to the edge of his underwear. She tugged at his underwear, pulling it down. His penis flopped out and she looked

152

away for a moment. The scratches disappeared
around to the other side of his leg as they moved
down his inner thigh just below his crotch. Jean
struggled with his body and managed to flip Billy over
in the tight confines of the back seat.

"Do you see anything?" Charlene asked.

Jean looked at the red scratches on Billy's butt.
The trail disappeared between the tight crevice of his
buttocks. She reached down with trembling fingers
and placed a hand on each buttock. She slowly pulled
his butt cheeks apart.

And then screamed the most frightening scream
ever heard on this desolate portion of road near
Arentown Pennsylvania.

"It's inside him. Oh my God, it's inside him."

"What is it?" Charlene craned her neck to look
into the backseat. Suddenly the car jerked to the side
and Charlene whipped her head back forward. She
was off the road, just on the edge of a ditch. She
whipped the wheel back to the left, narrowly avoiding
sending the car into the ditch. She slammed on the
brakes, sending Jean violently forward into the back
of the seat. Charlene unhooked her seat belt and spun
around in the driver's seat, leaning over into the back
seat.

The upper half of Billy's body had tumbled down
into the space between the front and back seat. His
buttocks stuck up in the air. The end of a dark tail
was visible just above his butt hole. The rest of the
creature was inside his rectum. Charlene could hear
the soft sounds of chewing. The leathery tail wiggled

excitedly.

Charlene threw the driver's side door open and bolted to the rear door. She yanked at the handle, but the door was locked. She slammed her palm against the window. "Open the door!"

Jean stared at her blankly.

Charlene again slammed her palm against the window. "Mom, open the door!"

Jean fumbled at the unlock button and finally managed to get the door unlocked. Charlene jerked the door open. "Move, Mom!" She elbowed her way past her mother and grabbed at the visible portion of the tail weaving and waving at her from Billy's butt. She pulled on the tail. For a moment, Charlene felt some resistance, but then she yanked on it sharply, tugging the creature out of her brother. A stench of feces assailed her nostrils and Charlene gagged.

Billy howled in pain.

Charlene whipped the creature out into the road, her face twisted in disgust, her hand still shaking as she let it fly from her fingers. The creature squealed as it hit the pavement. It regained its balance and sat in the middle of the road. It was about four inches tall and an inch or so wide, with what looked like a hard black shell on its back. It had a small oval head with round black eyes and a proboscis sticking out from its mouth area. It had what look liked six legs, three on each side of its body. It raised one of its forelegs to its proboscis and the tubular mouth part sucked at the feces covering its claw. Charlene thought of a dung beetle. A dung beetle with a tail like a rat. A dung beetle from hell that thrived on human feces.

And then the dung beetle raced forward, charging right back at them, its tail sticking straight up in the air.

Charlene bolted back to the car and dove into the driver's seat, slamming the door shut behind her. She turned to see the back door was still open. "Shut the door! Mom, shut the door!"

The dung beetle sped closer.

Jean fumbled at the door, but didn't close it in time. The dung beetle leaped into the backseat, going straight for Billy again. Jean shrieked and slammed at the beetle with her fist, knocking it away from Billy's leg. It fell to the ground behind the driver's side seat and Jean stomped at it. The beetle avoided her stomping feet and crawled back up Billy's leg, this time sinking its claws in deep. Billy whimpered, his face scrunching up in pain.

Charlene reached over the front seat and grabbed at the beetle, tugging at its shell. The bug sunk its claws even deeper into Billy's flesh. The strong stench of feces filled the car. "I can't get it off!"

Jean joined her struggle, grabbing at one of the beetle's legs, trying to wrench it free. Jean managed to pull one of the beetle's legs out from where it had hooked into Billy's skin. Blood oozed out of the cut from the incision the beetle had made when it sunk its claw into Billy's flesh. The beetle's leg was slick with Billy's blood and Jean lost her grip on the creature's appendage. The beetle sunk the claw back into Billy's leg, making a new puncture hole next to the bleeding cut.

Charlene let go of the beetle's shell and fumbled at her purse, pulling out her lighter. She flicked it repeatedly, trying to get a flame. She lunged back over the front seat, her body halfway into the back seat, and held the lighter next to the beetle's head, repeatedly flicking the lighter to keep the flame burning. The beetle finally relented under the assault of the fire on its head and released its grip, dropping to the floor.

"Stomp it!" Charlene shouted.

Jean stomped but still couldn't get a clean hit on the fast-moving beetle. The one time she struck it with her shoe, the beetle's hard shell deflected the blow. The beetle reared back and hissed a menacing hiss. Jean stared at the bug, momentarily paralyzed by the creature's vehement protest.

The beetle resumed its attack on Billy, clawing back up his leg towards his bare buttocks.

Charlene scrambled out of the car, but stopped as she saw a dozen dung beetles sitting on the side of the road. They were all standing on their rear hind legs, like miniature meerkats peering out over of their terrain.

Charlene composed herself and moved quickly for the open back door. She reached into the car and grabbed the beetle with both hands, tugging with all her might. She heard flesh tear and this time Bobby screamed in pain. She tugged harder and finally managed to disengage the creature from her brother's skin. Blood splashed across the back seat. Charlene whipped the beetle towards the other beetles standing on the side of the road. The other beetles scrambled away as the flung beetle twirled end over end towards them.

Suddenly, one of the other dung beetles on the side of the road erupted in an explosive mash of head, guts, legs, and shell. Then another one erupted into a mess of blood and guts.

"Get in your car!" Charlene heard a voice shout.

Charlene glanced around but could not find the source of the voice.

"Get in your car, you damn fool!"

Up. The voice was coming from somewhere above her. Charlene glanced up the rocky cliff wall that lined the road. She saw the glint of a rifle, and then she saw the man holding it. He put the gun to his eye and fired. Charlene started as she felt the bullet whizzing past her head and heard it whistle past her ear. Then she heard a very loud splat and she spun to see a dung beetle flopping on the ground only a few feet away from her. She shoved the back door shut and scrambled back into the front seat, pulling the door closed behind her.

A beetle slammed into the driver's side window with incredible force just as Charlene closed the door. The window cracked, but did not shatter. Charlene looked up to see another beetle flying towards the car. It folded its long wings beneath its shell and dive-bombed straight for the glass, picking up speed as it descended. It splattered against the glass. Another dung beetle crashed into the window. The cracks in the window widened.

More gunfire rang out, shot after shot echoing in the narrow canyon.

Charlene sat quietly in the car, forcing herself to stay calm, not knowing where to go, or what to do. She adjusted her glasses and tried not to scream.

They got the first aid kit out from under the passenger side seat and bandaged Billy up the best they could, disinfecting his cuts with first aid cream, then covering them with gauze and tape. The beetle attacks had finally tapered off and the sounds of gunfire had faded away. Charlene took advantage of the lull and hurried to work on Billy. She didn't know how the long the quiet interlude would last, or if the shooter would resume firing, but she knew she had to help her brother and get his wounds covered and get his bleeding under control. She had to do most of the work because her mother couldn't stop her hands from shaking. Neither one of them spoke as they worked on Billy. They soon ran out of gauze, so Charlene had to use folded up paper towels, along with the tape, to cover a few of the remaining smaller cuts in her brother's leg.

After they got his pants back on, Billy curled up in a corner of the back seat, his body trembling as he hugged his knees. His eyes were glassy, staring but seeing nothing.

"We need to go, Mom," Charlene said. She now sat in the driver's seat, her hand ready to turn on the ignition.

Jean nodded. She sat next to Billy in the back seat, putting a comforting arm on his leg. She looked up at her daughter. "Can you drive?"

"Yeah."

That's when a sharp knock sounded at the window by Charlene's head. Charlene bit back a scream and turned to see a man staring down at her from outside the car. He was dressed in a red and black flannel shirt and very worn denim jeans. He had dark hair, a long face, and a rounded chin. His eyes were a smoky grey, laced with a hint of red streaks. He held a rifle casually in one hand, the barrel pointing down to the road. She saw his lips move but she couldn't understand what he said. Charlene lowered the window a crack to hear him better.

"You can come out now," the man said. "They're gone."

"Thank you," Charlene finally managed to say. "I have to get my brother to a hospital. Do you know where the closest one is?"

The man took a step back away from the car and raised his rifle, pointing it straight at her. "I said you can come out now."

Charlene threw her hands up immediately, fighting back the fear threatening to overwhelm her. She forced herself to stay calm. "Okay, okay. Relax."

<hr/>

"What the hell are they?" Charlene asked. She and the man stood at the side of the road, looking down at the decimated bodies of the beetles Pernish had blasted with his rifle. Once she had gotten out of the car, he had lowered his rifle and his disposition had changed. His tone had become friendlier and less menacing. He introduced himself to her by simply saying, "I'm Pernish."

Pernish shook his head at her question. "Don't know. They started showing up a few weeks ago. They're everywhere now. I'm thinking that bug doctor caused it."

"Bug doctor?"

Pernish nodded. "Some guy living down the road a few miles from me. Experimenting on bugs. Trying to breed them. Trying to improve crop production or some shit." He shook his head. "I told him he shouldn't be playing God. Especially not with bugs.

Bugs are gonna outlast us anyway. No need to help them along. But he didn't listen. That's why I had to kill him."

Charlene froze for a moment, not sure if she had heard him correctly. He had said it so plainly, so casually. "You — you killed him?"

Pernish gave one slight nod. "The only thing that lets evil thrive is for good men to do nothing. So I done something. I ain't proud of it. But it needed to be done." He looked at her. "You think I was wrong doing that? Look what they done to yer brother. They already kilt four others."

Charlene was quiet for a long moment. She glanced back into the car. Her mother stared down at Billy, absently stroking his head. She was no help. She appeared to be in some kind of shocked state. Charlene looked back to Pernish. "Thank you for helping us."

"I try to warn people from coming here. Try and get 'em off the highway." He looked at her. "But sometimes people don't listen."

"Can you tell me where the nearest hospital is?"

"I could, but you're not going there."

"I have to get my brother to the hospital. He's bleeding."

Pernish peered into the back seat. Jean moved her body protectively in front of Billy, trying to shield her son from Pernish's gaze. "Nah," Pernish said. "He ain't bleeding no more. He'll be fine."

"I need to get to college," Charlene blurted out.

Pernish shook his head. "Not today, you don't."

"No." Charlene shook her head. "You don't understand. I have to get to college."

"No. You don't. Now that you are here, you need

to stay here and help me fight them."

Charlene continued to shake her head. "No, no. Just let us go. I need to get my brother to a hospital. We need to go."

Pernish shook his head in response to her. "I know where they live but I can't kill them all myself."

Charlene stared at him. "You're crazy." She blurted out the words, then immediately regretted them but knew she couldn't take them back.

Pernish scratched his head. "Maybe so." He paused for a moment. "I'll tell you what. You help me or I'll kill your mother and your little brother. How's that for crazy?"

<hr>

In the distance, a small house rested at the end of a winding dirt road. Pernish drove his battered pickup truck up the driveway and stopped before the house. "That's where he lived," Pernish said. "His lab's just beyond the house a bit."

"So why are we here?" Charlene asked. She sat beside Pernish in the truck. He had taken her purse from her, which contained her cell phone, so she had no way of calling for help.

Pernish put the truck in park and took the keys out of the ignition. "He left some notes. Maybe you smart college girl can figure them out. I'm not much of a reader."

"What about my mom and my brother?"

"We'll drop them at my house." Pernish glanced into the back seat of the truck. Billy and Jean were all trussed up, with their hands tied behind their backs, their feet bound. Dirty rags were tied tightly around their mouths to keep them quiet. Another dirty rag was tied around their eyes. Pernish looked back to Charlene. "They'll keep for now."

Charlene looked at the scribbled notes on the stained yellow legal pad she found on one of the desks. *Onthophagus caenobita is the only dung beetle species ever to have been found feeding on human feces.* She didn't know how to pronounce the Latin term, but that didn't matter. She adjusted her glasses and glanced around at the laboratory. It looked as if the scientist had been in the middle of dozens of other experiments. Most of the insects inside their glass cages were dead, probably of starvation, but a few of them were still alive. She stared at a praying mantis that moved slowly within its glass-walled confines. What the hell was he trying to do? She was too afraid to let any of the insects out of their glass cages. Who knew what kind of insanity the guy had bred into them. They would all just have to die.

Charlene thought about the notes she had read on the scientist's computer. His desktop computer had still been turned on; Pernish had not come back to the lab after he killed him, so everything was still just as it had been before Pernish took his life. There were all sorts of formulas and chemical compounds written everywhere, but there were also notes scribbled amidst all the equations. Terrifying notes. The jabberings of a lunatic. Talk of human population control. Rambling on about human extermination. She found lists of the insects that had the most poisonous venom, along with additional notes on how to augment the strength of their respective venoms to kill more people.

He really was a mad scientist.

"Any of that gibberish make sense to you?" Pernish asked.

Charlene nodded. Maybe Pernish didn't understand what was going on in a scientific sense, but she knew he understood what had been going on here was most assuredly evil. She softened her expression, letting the tightness in her jaw relax. Maybe Pernish was right to kill him. That was a horrible thought, but she couldn't shake it. "He was genetically modifying insects."

Pernish just looked at her.

"He was trying to turn bugs into weapons of mass destruction."

"I told you he was a bad fella."

Charlene looked at Pernish. "I think you were right." She glanced around the lab and looked back to Pernish. "Did you call the cops about all this?"

Pernish shook his head. "Me and the sheriff don't see eye to eye on things. Got us a bit of a checkered past, so to speak. He won't take kindly to me killing someone in his territory. Best we just handle this ourselves."

Charlene motioned to the lab with a wide sweep of her arms. "This is a pretty big deal, Pernish. We need to tell somebody. The FBI. Homeland Security. Somebody."

"I reckon I'll get around to that soon. But first we gotta stop these things from spreading, don't you think? We gotta stop them now."

"If we call Homeland Security, they'll probably be here in an hour."

"No."

"Why the hell not?" Charlene asked, her tone rising with a hint of agitation.

"Because I ain't got no papers."

"No papers?"

Pernish shook his head. "No birth certificate. No social security number. My momma just squirt me out and left me for dead. The Caldwells raised me up. They ain't much for paperwork, neither."

"Does the sheriff know this? That you don't have — an identity?"

Pernish squinted at her. "What're you blabbering about? I got an identity. I'm Pernish."

"I mean does he know you don't have a birth certificate?"

Pernish nodded. "Oh, he knows."

"And he didn't do anything about it?" Charlene asked.

"He had a soft spot for the Caldwells. Old man Elmor saved his life once, so he cashed in on the favor. He just let me be, long as I don't make no more trouble." Pernish paused. "But now I done made trouble so I'm not looking forward to seeing the sheriff any time soon."

Charlene was quiet for a moment. "Where are they? The Caldwells. Let's get the Caldwells to help us."

Pernish shook his head. "Not unless you know how to raise the dead." He looked at Charlene. "Relax, I didn't kill them. They died of old age years and years ago."

Charlene said nothing.

"You done jabberin' now?" Pernish asked. "Can we get to work?"

The bucket of feces in the back seat of the truck reeked to high heaven. Pernish didn't seemed bothered by it at all. He slowed his battered pickup truck to a stop and pointed out the dirty, scratched front window of the vehicle. "They're in there."

Charlene followed his gaze to see a small cave visible just beyond a clump of bushes. The opening was about two feet tall and maybe three feet wide, carved into the side of a small hill. Charlene stared at the small dark hole.

"You need to go in there," Pernish said.

"*I* need to go in there?"

Pernish nodded. "I can't fit. I already tried."

"You think I can fit in there?"

"Sure. You or your little brother. Don't matter none to me who goes in there, long as the job gets done."

Charlene stared at the cave entrance for a long moment. She adjusted her glasses. "What am I supposed to do when I get in there?"

"Kill them all." He looked at her with a frown. "You sure you're ready for college?"

Charlene ignored his question. She had no desire to argue with the man.

Pernish clambered out the truck, grabbing his rifle, and moved to the front of the vehicle.

Charlene climbed out and moved over to him. She looked back to the cave. "So what do I do?"

"First thing we gotta do is cork up your butt hole so they can't get in," Pernish said.

"You touch me and I'll scratch your eyes out."

Pernish shook his head.

"What?" The word came out in a sharp snap.

"Can you keep your trap shut longer than five minutes at a time?" Pernish asked. "See, cause if they can't get in through your bottom, they'll go in through your big fat mouth and dig their way down through your intestines."

Charlene opened her mouth to retort back, but then clamped her lips shut. She pushed her glasses back into place.

Pernish handed her an oil-stained rag. "Here, use this."

Charlene stared at the filthy piece of cloth, then looked back up to Pernish. "Are you out of your mind? I am not putting that anywhere near me."

"Suit yourself." Pernish wiped his nose with the rag and shoved it back into his back pocket.

Charlene took off one of her shoes, careful not to touch the ground with her foot as she did so, and removed her ankle sock. It was relatively clean. She had just put on a fresh pair that very morning. It would have to do. She looked up to see Pernish watching her curiously. "Do you mind?"

"Nope. I don't mind at all." He continued to watch her.

She unbuttoned her jeans and tried to shove the ankle sock down her backside, but her jeans were too tight. She looked up at Pernish. "My jeans are too tight. They can't get in there."

Pernish looked at her. "You think your brother'd say the same thing?"

She looked up at Pernish. "Turn around. Don't be a perv."

Pernish turned away from her.

Charlene wriggled her jeans down, moving them

down to her thighs. Her underwear got caught in the jeans and slid down to her thighs along with her pants. She stuffed the sock down between her butt cheeks, trying to block her anus as best she could.

"How come you ain't got no hair down there?"

She looked up to see Pernish staring down between her exposed thighs. She quickly snatched at her underwear, drawing them back up. She tugged at her jeans, wriggling them back up into place. She snapped the button on her jeans and glared at Pernish. "That was rude."

Pernish shook his head. "Not answering my question is rude." He looked at her. "Ain't never seen no bald cunny before."

"And you never will again."

"Oh, I'm thinkin' I might."

"Are you threatening to rape me? Because I will kill you before that happens. I will scratch your fucking eyes out and rip your dick right off your body."

Pernish cocked his head ever so slightly. "I'm not liking the tone in your voice, young lady. And I don't like you accusing me of something that ain't true. I ain't no rapist."

Charlene just stared at him.

"I was just thinking you might want to show your appreciation for saving your family. A little happy time amongst friends."

"A little happy time?"

Pernish nodded. "Sure. Doing that makes me happy. Don't it make you happy?"

Charlene held up her hand. "Okay, we need to stop this conversation right now and concentrate on the task at hand."

Pernish was quiet for a moment. "Speakin' of bald cunnies, you'd best plug up that other hole, too." He slowly turned to face away from her.

"Spread it out around the opening, off to the side over there. We need to draw out as many as we can before you go in," Pernish said.

Charlene stared at the contents of the bucket, her nose wrinkling at the foul smell.

Pernish frowned at her. "Get over it, college girl. It's your own shit. Now just wipe some around the area."

Charlene grabbed a large stick from the ground and stuck it into the bucket. She smeared the brown goo over some nearby rocks, and along the ground. She plopped a glob of it off to the right of the cave. She fought back a gag.

It didn't take long for the dung beetles to take the bait.

"Get back! There's one!"

Charlene started at Pernish's cry and froze for a moment.

"Damn it, girl, get back!"

She looked over at the cave entrance to see a dung beetle poke its head out of the darkness. It scurried over to some of the bait she had just smeared on the rocks and started feeding on the shit with its long proboscis. Charlene regained her senses and moved, hurrying back over to Pernish, moving behind him. "Shoot it," she whispered with an urgency in her voice.

"Not yet."

Another beetle appeared, then another. Soon, a dozen dung beetles were feeding on the bait she had laid out, their tails wiggling excitedly as they ate her feces.

Pernish opened fire, killing six of the beetles in a matter of seconds. The guts of one of the blown-away beetles splashed across another beetle, disturbing its feeding. The beetle raised up on its hind legs and hissed in the direction the invasive splash of guts had come from. Pernish blasted away its midsection with a well-aimed shot.

Charlene grit her teeth, biting back a jubilant shout. Kill those fuckers. Kill them all.

Pernish quickly took out three more beetles, sending a bullet straight up the rear of one of them. The bullet ripped through the beetle and erupted out of the insect's head, blowing tiny bug brains in all directions.

Two of the dung beetles scurried back into the cave.

And then everything was quiet again.

"Well," Pernish said. "That wasn't many, but at least we got a few more."

❦

Pernish finished tying the rope tightly around Charlene's waist. "You tug on this three times and I'll pull you right out."

Charlene nodded. The socks blocking her anus and her vagina rubbed uncomfortably against her beneath her jeans. She had a sudden need to pee, but fought back the urge. As an extra layer of protection, more cords of rope were tied tightly around the bottom of each of her pant legs to hopefully prevent any dung beetles from crawling up her legs.

Pernish stuck a lighter in her front pocket, then slid a second lighter into her back pocket. "Just go in as deep as you can and start pouring. Spread the gas around as much as you can, then tug on the rope twice. I'll start pulling you out. That's when you need to light it up. Once you see the pool of gas all lit up, then you tug on the rope three times and I'll yank you out." He looked at Charlene. "We clear on the plan?"

"Can't we just pour the gas around the opening or something?" Charlene asked.

Pernish shook his head. "I don't know how deep that cave goes. You need to find that out."

"Can't we just use a flame thrower or something?"

Pernish frowned at her. "A flame thrower? You think I'm made of money or something?" He looked at the ground and shook his head as if that were the most foolish thing he had ever heard.

"This doesn't seem very safe," Charlene said.

Pernish pursed his lips. "You know what else ain't safe? Your mama and your brother sitting all tied up at my house. Who knows if those things will get to them before we get back." He looked off in the distance, then turned back to stare at Charlene. "You ready?"

Charlene grabbed the five gallon jug full of gasoline that was sitting on the ground next to them and raised it up, along with the small flashlight she held in her other hand. "No, but let's fucking get this over with anyway."

The cave was dark and wet, and reeked worse than an overflowing porta-potty on a hot summer day. Charlene gagged every few breaths, but forced herself to continue on. The cave was low and narrow. She had to push the gasoline jug in front of her, then army crawl forward behind it. She kept repeating that process as she moved deeper and deeper into the cave.

She raised the flashlight up and shined the light deeper into the cave. The lenses on her glasses were covered with smears now, but she could still see through them. The ground was slick with feces, the walls shiny with some kind of disgusting residue. She hadn't seen any dung beetles yet.

Until one came scurrying out of the darkness in front of her and crawled right into her mouth. She immediately tried to spit it out, but the beetle latched itself onto her tongue. Charlene howled in pain, trying to spit out the infernal insect, but the beetle held on tight. She chomped down on the bug and heard a sickening crunch in her mouth as she bit the beetle in half. She felt a warm splash of dung beetle guts flood her mouth. She spit and spit and spit, desperately trying to force any of the beetle's remains out of her mouth. The taste made her gag and she vomited in her mouth, then spit out the hot vile liquid. Some of it dribbled down her chin.

Another dung beetle moved towards her mouth, but she swatted it away with the flashlight. The insect quickly resumed its attack, moving straight for her face. She raised the flashlight with what little ceiling room she had and brought the end of the flashlight down hard on the dung beetle, crushing its shell and smearing its entrails all over the cave floor.

Charlene felt something crawling on the back of her calf and she shook her leg, trying to dislodge it. Her mind raced and swelled in sheer panic. She fought to catch her breath. She felt more movement on her legs and she just knew the dung beetles were starting to clamber all over her. She tried to spit away the sourness that coated the inside of her mouth, but the foul taste lingered. She spit up another mouthful of vomit. Her head started to pound.

She thought of her mom and her brother and forced herself to keep going. She crawled further into the cave. Her glasses were smeared with feces, but she knew trying to wipe them clean would only make it worse. Charlene shined her flashlight deeper into the tight tunnel and saw hundreds of dung beetles gathered at the end of the cave. They were all busy feeding on an enormous ball of shit. That was enough; she couldn't take any more. She fumbled at the gas cap on the jug and managed to loosen it quickly, swatting the black piece of plastic away once it got loose enough. She dumped the gas can over and its contents spilled out into the cave. The heavy scent of gasoline was a welcome respite from the thick stench of feces that filled the cave.

Charlene reached behind her back to pull the lighter out of her pocket and felt the stinging hook of a dung beetle's claw stabbing into the hand that held the flashlight. She yelped in pain and swatted her hand quickly, trying to dislodge the beetle. The beetle clung tightly to her hand. She flung her hand upwards, smashing the beetle against the ceiling of the cave repeatedly, finally dislodging the creature. This violent motion cracked the flashlight lens and the light flickered twice, then went out, plunging her into darkness.

She nearly went mad with fear, but forced herself not to scream. She panted hot breaths, doing her best to stay calm but knowing full well she was on the verge of losing her sanity. The lighter. Get the lighter. Burn these fuckers all to hell. Charlene fumbled in her back pocket with her left hand, ignoring the stinging pain in her right hand, and drew out the lighter. She brought the lighter in front of her and flicked it on. The pale flame revealed hundreds of dung beetles looking straight at her. Their eyes glistened with a dark menace, like a sea of glittering death stones, all of them promising her eternal damnation. It was the scariest thing she had even seen in her life. She felt herself release a stream of urine, unable to control it.

The flame went out and she quickly started to back away, shuffling backwards as quickly as she could, driving her elbows into the ground and pushing herself back, grunting and panting hard with the effort. She flicked the lighter on again and saw the beetles were nearly on top of her, dozens and dozens of them scurrying towards her. She put the flame to the ground and the spilled gasoline in front of her immediately went up in flames, singeing her hand, the flames leaping up to burn her face, catching her shirt on fire.

The rope. Tug on the rope!

"Pull me out! Pernish, pull me out!" she yelled, yanking on the rope as best she could. She didn't stop at three yanks. She kept tugging and pulling at the rope again and again and again. Fire crackled and popped all around her.

She felt herself getting jerked backwards. Charlene watched the end of the cave erupt into a massive ball of fire. Then her head cracked sharply against a rock and the blazing mass of bright flames turned into a cold blackness.

Charlene opened her eyes to see a blurry vision of her mother and brother sitting at a table, eating a meal with Pernish.

"Hey, she's awake," Billy said.

Jean and Billy set their forks down and hurried over to her.

Charlene felt something on her face and reached up to feel some gauze covering her cheek. She touched it and winced. The burn was hot and painful.

"You okay?" Jean asked.

"I think so," Charlene said. "What happened?"

"You killed all those suckers," Billy said.

Charlene looked at her brother, then looked over to Pernish. He was a bit of a blur, but she could still make him out. Pernish nodded at her. She sat up, wincing at the pain in her head. She reached up to feel a bit fat welt on her head. She glanced down and noticed she was wearing a fresh shirt and clean jeans. She vaguely remembered pissing on herself in the cave. She was grateful that someone had cleaned her up. A nagging smell of feces still lingered in her nose, though.

"Me and Pernish went out to check. Not one of them came out of the cave," Billy added.

"Where's my glasses?" Charlene asked.

"All burned up in the cave, I reckon," Pernish said. "You didn't have 'em on when I tugged you out."

Jean handed Charlene some ice cubes wrapped up

in a cloth. "Here. Put this on that."

Charlene took the cloth and gingerly placed it against the bump on her head. The cold felt good on her wound. She looked over to her brother. "You okay?"

"Yeah, I'll be all right. Kinda hurts still, but I'll be okay."

"You see a doctor?" Charlene asked Billy.

Billy shook his head. "Nah, I'll be okay."

Charlene looked over to her mother, but Jean said nothing. She looked back to Billy. "How long was I out?"

"About half a day or so."

Charlene slowly got to her feet and moved over to Pernish. She reached down to where he sat at the table and kissed his cheek. "Thanks for pulling me out." She should have been furious at him for putting her in that position in the first place, but now all she could feel was gratitude towards him for saving her life. She could have easily died in that cave if he hadn't gotten her out.

Pernish smiled at her. "It's okay. Your momma done give me what I wanted. We shared a little happy time together."

Charlene frowned. She looked over at the blurry face of her mother, but Jean avoided looking at her.

"Time for you to get to college, ain't it?" Pernish asked.

They stopped at a hotel in New Jersey. They were all too tired to go any farther. None of them had the energy to unpack. They would get to New York in the morning and start fresh.

"I think I pooped out a baby beetle," Billy said from inside the hotel bathroom.

Jean was out getting them some food, so Charlene went into the bathroom. She didn't even look. She was actually grateful her vision was shitty without her glasses. She just flushed the toilet. She didn't want to look. She didn't want to know. Out of sight, out of mind. And out of her mind was where she was going to go if she saw one more of those damned cursed dung beetles in her life.

※━❄〖⑨〗❄━※

The baby dung beetles moved through the four inch pipe that connected the hotel room's toilet to the larger six inch pipe that served the toilet system of the entire hotel. Unbeknownst to Billy, he had defecated more than a dozen tiny baby beetles, not just one. They rode the current in the six inch pipe where they then joined a much wider flow through a larger pipe that served the entire neighborhood.

It didn't take long for them to reach the waste treatment plant. Coarse metal screens filtered out bigger chunks of debris such as paper, rags, and leaves. A few of the baby dung beetles got trapped and eventually perished as they depleted the stored oxygen they had been using during their travels in the current, but most of the tiny bugs easily moved through the gaps in the mesh.

A few more of them died as their journey continued to the grit chamber, where sand, dirt, and inorganic solids settled. Some of the baby dung beetles let their bodies settle to the bottom and died, unable to fight the current any longer. The remaining other baby dung beetles were collected, along with all the other chunks of debris and gritty stuff, and shipped off to the local landfill.

Most of the baby dung beetles didn't survive the entire journey from Billy's buttocks to the local landfill, but a few of them did. And they were very hungry.

TERRORSTORY #28
THE TINIES

Guy Karlyle burst into the building, a grim frown darkening his face. He was late. Again. God damn it! Every fucking time he needed to be in the office for a meeting, he was late. Every fucking time. Traffic jams on I-89. Gaper's block because of a rollover accident on the exit ramp at Wilson Street. A fire closing Harris Road. A torrential downpour with raindrops fatter than golf balls making traffic slow to a tortoise crawl. Snow so thick it was like cotton balls being spit down out of the sky from an army of pissed off angels, forcing every car on the road to move two inches an hour. Faulty starter on his car; he missed the entire day because of that one, let alone the meeting. It was always something. Always fucking something.

He stabbed the elevator button with his finger. Guy was in his early twenties, with close-cropped blond hair that worked well with his lean, angular face. He fidgeted while the numbers above the door slowly glowed white. They were going up from 8 to 9 to 10. Shit, it was still going up. He looked over to his right at the second elevator. The 3 indicator was lit up and the down arrow was illuminated. It was only a few floors above him and heading down to the main floor he was on. He shifted over in front of the second elevator with a lithe sidestep leap.

He needed to make this meeting. The entire Duyos presentation was dependent on him starting it off with his numbers. He had stayed up all night preparing his PowerPoint slides. And the numbers looked good. Sales were up for the first quarter and heading into the second quarter with a strong thrust. He purposely made the second slide graphic look like a big dick standing at attention. Jenny was probably the only one who'd notice. She had as twisted a sense of perverted humor as he did.

Guy felt confident that his presentation would push the Duyos client into spending more money in the second quarter after they saw the momentum their marketing initiatives had built in the first quarter. And after that horny old bitty running the Duyos company saw the big fat cock slide he made, he knew that would clinch it. Guy mentally snorted at his own subliminal brilliance. They'd be fools to let that momentum slide and let their competitors have a chance to steal some of their market share. They needed to ramp it up and step on their competitors' throats. They need to keep their dicks hard. His presentation laid that all out, with an undeniable call to action for the Duyos company to increase their marketing budget. And thus earn him a nice tidy bonus.

The elevator on his left continued up. 21. 22. Guy looked at the floor indicator bar above the second elevator he now stood in front of. The 2 glowed softly. Then, the 2 dimmed. Come on, come on. He glanced at his watch. He fidgeted from foot to foot. Come on! He looked left. The first elevator continued to move upwards. 37. 38. It was stopping on nearly every other floor. That elevator would take forever to come back down.

I should have emailed the ppt file to Jenny, Guy thought as he fingered the USB drive in his left pocket. Too late now. Besides, he was the one supposed to be presenting it. He didn't want to give away his work to anyone else, anyway. Fuck it. I did all the damn work. I should be the one presenting it.

After what felt like hours, Guy heard the elevator car in the bank in front of him arrive with a loud grinding noise. Fucking finally! The elevator door opened and he leaped inside.

Guy stabbed at the button for the 26th floor. Come on, come on! He saw a woman approaching the elevator with a raised hand and a beseeching look on her face. He quickly stabbed at the Close Door button. The doors started to close and the woman gave him one of the darkest glares he had ever seen. She looked royally pissed. He saw her pull something out of her purse and point it at him. What the fuck? It looked like some kind of stun gun at first, but then he realized it was too small. It was like some kind of remote control or something. He tried to focus on what she was holding, but then the elevator doors closed before he could get a good look at what was in her hand, and the elevator moved with a grinding lurch.

Guy glanced at his watch. Five minutes. Shit, it was gonna be close. It was gonna be damn close. He looked at the numbers above the door. The L illuminated. What? No, it was still going down! No, no, no! Shit. He stabbed at the 26th floor button, then the 27th, the 28th, the 29th. No, up! I need to go up, you piece of shit.

The B illuminated. Then the B dimmed.

The elevator continued moving downward. For a moment, Guy felt a swirling mass of confusion. He scowled deeply. What the fuck? He jabbed at the 26th floor button again repeatedly even though it was still lit.

Then the elevator stopped. The doors remained closed. Guy just stared at their dull grey metal surface. Movement caught his eye and he looked down to see a thin wisp of smoke seep into the elevator cage from beneath the doors. Fire. That was the first thing he thought of. Shit, the building was on fire!

He was about to shout an alarm when the elevator doors opened. He pushed himself against the back wall of the elevator, throwing his hands up in front of his face, expecting a blast of heat or even flames to come bursting into the elevator and fry him alive. But there was no blast of heat. No flames. The air felt cool, almost cold.

Outside the elevator, the hallway was dim, illuminated by a few yellowing bulbs hanging from fixtures in the concrete ceiling. Guy stood motionless, pressed against the back wall of the elevator. Then, he jerked forward and jabbed random buttons on the door panel. He jabbed the Close Door button, but the doors did not close. He hit the Emergency Stop button, but that did nothing. No alarm blared.

Guy reached into his right pocket for his smartphone, but his pocket was empty. He searched his pockets, patting his body everywhere. Shit, it wasn't here. All he had was his keys and the USB drive, and his wallet in his back pocket. Where the hell is my phone? Then, he stopped. He remembered. It was on the front seat of his car. He had taken it out and plugged it into the USB port in his car to charge it. He had forgotten to grab it when he raced out of his car to try and make it to the meeting on time. Son of a bitch.

Then he heard noises. Noises coming from outside the elevator, from down the hallway. Buzzing noises, like some machine being operated. Guy peered out into the murky gloom. "Hey," he said weakly. Then he made his voice stronger, louder. "Hey, anybody down here? The elevator is stuck."

No answer.

Guy took a hesitant step out of the elevator. And then another and another, moving slowly down the dim corridor, keeping his gaze focused in front of him. "Anybody down here? The goddamn elevator is out of whack." He took a few more steps into the gloomy hall. He heard a grating sound and turned around to see the elevator doors crushing closed behind him with a resounding thud. He quickly raced back towards the elevator bank and threw his hands against the doors. "No, wait!" He searched the wall for a button, but there was none. The wall was smooth. There was no elevator button panel. He pounded on the elevator doors. "Wait!"

The low buzzing sound caused him to freeze. It grew louder behind him. Guy slowly turned his head to look over his shoulder.

The corridor was filled with a low fog that hung just above the concrete floor, the white haze a few feet tall. He slowly turned fully around to stared out into the murky gloom beyond the elevator doors. The white haze reminded him of the fog at Giorgio's, except this hallway wasn't full of pulsating disco lights and beautiful women dressed in slinky outfits.

The buzzing sound came out of the gloom. It sounded louder now. Closer.

Guy quickly glanced around the area. He had a sudden need to be holding something in his hands. Something. Anything. Anything he could use as a weapon. The wall to his right was just bare concrete. There was no fire extinguisher box attached to the wall as he had hoped there would be. No axe. Nothing but a wall of stone. To his left, a thick row of piping ran along the wall, disappearing into the stone wall near him. Some kind of water pipe or electrical conduit, probably. Guy followed the piping down the corridor with his gaze; the piping faded into the gloom dozens of feet down the narrow hallway. There was nothing to grab. No loose piping. No stray tools left by a maintenance worker. Nothing but an empty corridor laced with a layer of fog.

How the fuck can there be a layer of fog in the sub-basement? How is that even possible? It's not, he realized. It's just not possible. Is this the most lucid fucking dream I've ever had? But he knew he wasn't dreaming. He was awake and this was really happening to him.

The buzzing sound rang out again. It was even louder this time. Closer. It sounded like an engine accelerating. Then a dark shape appeared in the gloom. It was low to the ground, but its dark shape was still visible above the layer of fog. Guy felt his heart seize in his chest. Jesus, what the hell is that? Is that some kind of huge bug? He hated bugs. He hated spiders. He hated mosquitoes. He hated roaches. He hated bees. He hated moths. He hated flies. He didn't discriminate. He hated them all. He looked at the thing in the hallway. It was some kind of insect-thing he had never seen before. And it was moving ever so slowly closer to him.

Guy glanced around the area, but nothing magically appeared. No weapon miraculously dropped out of the ceiling. A loose wrench didn't suddenly appear on the cement floor. He rubbed his hand through his hair. He shoved his hand into his pocket and pulled out his key ring. There was nothing on there but his house key and his car key fob. Not much of a weapon but it was better than just a bare fist.

The bug thing moved closer. Guy didn't see any visible wings on the creature, but it was somehow hovering in the air, gliding slowly towards him. One cyclopean black eye covered half of it surface. The rest of its rounded body had a metallic sheen to it, like the June beetles that he used to fish out of his backyard swimming pool.

My belt! I can use it like a whip. He quickly unhooked his belt and yanked it out of the loops, ripping one of them with the violent jerking action. His pants sagged a few inches, but held up. He gripped his keys in one hand, sticking the sharp edges out between his fingers, and clutched his belt in the other.

The flying bug thing moved closer.

"Heeyah, get out of here!" Guy snapped the belt at the bug, trying to use it like a whip.

The bug thing wasn't fazed. It easily evaded the whipping belt and buzzed closer. It stopped a few feet from him. Its big black eye stared at him. Guy lurched forward and stabbed his key tips down at the bug thing, puncturing its black eye. The bug thing's eye shattered like it was a piece of glass. No blood gushed out. No liquid at all. He could immediately see wires and circuits and electronic components visible within the shattered eye socket. It wasn't a bug. It's a robot, he thought. Or a goddamn mini drone or something.

The drone suddenly turned and buzzed back down the corridor.

Guy didn't know why, but he had an irresistible urge to give chase, so he raced after it.

Guy leaned his back against the cold stone of the corridor wall, took a deep breath, then peered around the corner again.

It was still there. A shimmering portal of some kind. He had seen the drone fly through it, but it had not come back out again. The portal looked as if it was just hanging in the air, floating in the corridor a foot off the ground. It was the source of all the fog; the misty whiteness drifted out of the circular opening. It was small, only a few feet in diameter. Just large enough for several of the bug thing drones to fit through, but far too small for him to fit through.

He pulled back to lean against the corridor wall again. Now what? You just have to know, don't you? The voice inside his head urged him to find out more. Guy fought back the urge, but he knew he was going to lose that battle. He had to know what it was. He had to get closer. He pushed himself off the wall and stepped around the corner of the corridor. He stood a few feet from the portal, standing very still, watching it. The fog pooled around his feet. He still clutched his belt in one hand and his key ring in the other. He dropped his belt because he felt like he needed at least one free hand in case something crazy happened that he needed to react to. He put the keys back between his fingers on his right hand, their sharp metal ends pointing out away from his knuckles.

Guy stepped closer to the portal. He paused, waiting for some kind of reaction, but nothing happened. He continued moving closer. He reached the portal and stopped. He stooped and reached his left hand down towards the portal. His fingers reached the shimmering edge and he kept moving them forward, sinking his hand into the portal. He quickly jerked his hand back out and studied his fingers. They appeared normal. He squeezed them. They felt fine. No tingling. No weird temperature fluctuation. They felt completely normal.

Don't do it, don't do it, don't you fucking do it. The warning voice in his mind screamed at him not to do what he was thinking about doing.

But he did it.

Guy moved down to his knees to get closer to the opening, and stuck his head into the portal.

At first, Guy had difficulty comprehending what he was seeing, but then things started to take shape and come into focus. He stared into some kind of interstellar space. There were hundreds of vessels lined up in a row right near his head. It looked like some kind of armada was assembled. He looked into the distance and saw row after row after row of the vessels. He thought they were miles away because they were so small, but then realized they were only a few feet away from him.

And then he realized he wasn't able to breathe. Guy jerked his head back out of the portal, gasping for a breath. He panted for a few moments, getting his breathing under control. What the hell was that? An alien invasion force? It looked like there were tens of thousands of them. Hundreds of thousands. Maybe even millions. He couldn't tell. The endless space was filled with them, stretching into the distance as far as he could see. Millions of tiny flying saucers.

He stuck his hand back through the portal, reaching to his left where he had seen the vessels closest to the opening. He wanted to grab one and take a closer look at it. He cried out suddenly and withdrew his hand. A burnt smoldering hole was visible in his palm. "Son of a bitch!" he snarled. The wound was charred around the edges, the intensity of whatever heat blast struck him cauterizing the wound. Some blood still seeped out around the edges of the wound. They shot me, he realized with a growing rage. They fucking shot me.

Guy snarled and shoved his hand back into the portal, grabbing wildly. His fingers hit something and he immediately latched onto it, gripping it tight. He jerked his hand back out of the portal and looked down at what he held in his hand. It was a small object about the size of a matchbox. It was some kind of flying saucer, he thought again. A miniature spaceship. He could see a projecting gun barrel start to glow red and he instinctively knew it was powering up. Probably to shoot him again. He tossed the tiny ship to the ground and stomped on it. It crunched nicely under his heel.

He shoved his hand into the portal and flung about wildly, groping, grabbing anything his fingers touched. He pulled out another ship and quickly smashed it under his shoe. He pulled out another, then another and another, smashing them all under his heel. He pulled out another ship, but this one managed to get a shot off and it grazed Guy's skull, singeing his flesh. "Son of a bitch," he growled and whipped the tiny vessel against the stone wall. It crumpled and crashed to the ground, sparking as it fell.

Guy stood still for a moment, his breathing hot and heavy. What if there were a million of these things waiting on the other side? Even though they were small, he realized the magnitude of the damage they could do. It would be like a million ships filling the sky and firing deadly laser beams. By itself, an individual ship wasn't so frightening, but the sheer quantity of them would be overwhelming.

Suddenly, four ships buzzed out of the portal, their tiny guns blazing. He got hit twice in the arm, the hot beams singeing his clothes, burning his skin. Guy yelped in pain as the razor-sharp blasts slashed him. One beam sliced a burn across his cheek, leaving an ugly searing black mark across his flesh.

Guy swatted at the ships, hitting one of them with a lucky swing. It spun out of control and smashed into the concrete wall in a tiny explosion of metal. He snatched his belt off the floor and whipped the leather strip wildly about. He hit another ship and it teetered, then crashed to the ground. Another laser blast struck his shoulder, spinning him around as pain flared through him. Guy threw his belt down and snatched one of the ships right out of the air. He stared at his closed palm, feeling the ship slamming against his fingers, trying to get free of his hold. Then a laser blast burst through one of his fingers. "Motherfucker!" He whipped the ship to the ground and stomped on it.

The fourth ship hit him in the shoulder and Guy howled as his flesh smoked from the strike. He spun, flailing his arms about. The ship dodged his wild strikes and fired again, hitting him in the thigh. His leg buckled and he dropped to one knee.

Guy grabbed the leather tip of his belt and whipped it upwards. The metal of the buckle hit the edge of the ship, sending it careening into the concrete wall. The ship hit the wall, but then recovered, turning back to face him. Guy quickly grabbed the vessel and whipped it to the floor, wasting no time in stomping on it. Pain flared hotly in his wounded thigh.

Guy fought to catch his breath. Numerous black gouges marred his flesh across his shoulders, arms, and his leg. His fingers throbbed. The flesh on his thigh still smoked from the last hit.

He looked at two of the smashed ships on the ground. He clenched his teeth and bent over to snatch them up. He hurried over to the portal, wincing as he moved awkwardly on his wounded leg, and shoved two of the smashed ships back through the portal. "Take that, you little fuckers." He quickly gathered up another one of the fallen ships and shoved it back into the portal. That'll show 'em who's boss, he thought.

Guy grimaced as he stared at the portal. What the hell just happened? Was that some kind of new Russian weapon? Some kind of tunnel through space? Some kind of crazy terrorist shit? His entire body was wracked with pain. Was this really the precursor of an alien invasion?

He heard a soft metallic clicking noise and looked down to see one of the ships laying on the ground. Its hull was dented but it still appeared to have power. Its tiny gun barrels were smashed, now useless. A small red light pulsed on one end of the tiny vessel. Guy reached down and picked up the tiny ship.

Behind him in the distance, Guy heard the faint sound of an elevator ding. His eyes went wide and he spun around, racing back down the corridor. He could hear the sound of the elevator doors sliding open. He rounded the corner and raced for the open elevator doors.

Then the doors started to close.

Guy tried to run faster, but his wounded thigh slowed his pace. He panted as he raced towards the doors, his face filled with desperation, his hand reaching out beseechingly. "No!"

He managed to thrust his hand into the small gap between the doors just before they closed, and the doors re-opened. He staggered into the elevator and slammed into one of the walls, breathing hard. He jabbed at the 26th floor button. The elevator doors closed.

Guy watched the row of numbers above the door start to light up as the elevator ascended. His leg ached and his face ached and his fingers ached and his shoulder ached. He reached up and gingerly touched the burn on his cheek, wincing as he touched the scorched flesh on his face. Images of the portal and the attacking ships filled his head. Was it some kind of fucked up terrorist techno-weapon? Some new nano-technology-powered weapon?

The 26th floor button lit up and the doors opened. Guy stared at the bustling scene before him. Two well-dressed men walked by, absorbed in the contents of a folder one of them carried. Jenny sat at a nearby desk, busy re-stocking her printer with paper. Several more of his co-workers sat in nearby cubicles, working on their desktops. "Umm, Halloween was last month," Serena quipped as she strolled past him.

Just then, Mr. Markel walked by the elevator. He was the head of their Midwestern office, the vice president of Markel Marketing, dressed sharply in a dark blue suit and a so-tight-to-his-neck-he-should-be-choking tie. He paused to stare at Guy, his stern face filling with obvious disapproval and blatant disgust.

"Mr. Markel, you have to listen to what just happened," Guy said. He took a step forward, hitching up his beltless pants with his bleeding fingers as he moved, but the cold glare of his big boss staring at him made Guy pause. He didn't even make it out of the elevator.

"No, I don't," Markel said.

"No, really. You have to listen. I was in the elevator and it brought me down—"

Markel raised his hand, his face contorted in utter disdain. "Karlyle, just shut up."

"No! You have to listen to me! There's something in the basement. You have to send somebody down there!"

"Karlyle, I don't have to listen to you. In fact, I never want to hear your voice ever again. We lost the Duyos account because of you. You're fired. Don't bother packing up your desk. We'll do it for you." Markel looked over to Jenny. "Jenny, get security on the phone. Make sure this pathetic idiot gets escorted out of the building."

Guy looked at Jenny. She was a pretty girl with red hair and green eyes. They had dated once, but didn't really hit it off. Still, he considered her a friend. He looked pleadingly at her. She immediately looked away from him and started dialing. Guy frowned.

Markel reached over and hit the elevator button. The elevator doors closed.

Guy stared blankly at the steel wall of the elevator doors in front of him. Fired. God damn it. I need this job. That mother fucker. Guy ground his teeth. Damn it! He felt every muscle in his body tense, adding a layer of agony on top of the physical pain he was already feeling. How the hell am I going to pay my rent? Son of a bitch!

And then he felt an odd tingling inside him. Guy suddenly felt very light headed, and staggered. He hit the wall of the elevator with his shoulder, but managed to stay on his feet. He look at his charred hand. Did they inject him with something when they shot him? Had they poisoned him? He stood there for a long moment, blinking rapidly, trying to clear his swimming vision. The dizziness faded and his mind cleared.

Guy opened his other hand to stare at the small vessel he still clutched in his palm. A faint red light pulsated from within the damaged vessel somewhere, giving the ship a soft red glow. There was something still alive in the vessel. He wasn't sure how he knew, but he just did. He also knew this wasn't the end of it.

He looked closer at the pulsing light. It wasn't just pulsing at the same interval. The light was changing, growing bright, then dim, the pulse brief one time, then lasting a moment longer the next. It was communicating. The ship was sending him a message. And he understood it. Somehow, he understood it. The entities in the ship told Guy they had been studying his kind through Earth's communications systems. They were hidden in surveillance systems, buried in communication centers, spying through web cams, surfing the wifi waves, riding on the tails of every email message sent, spreading themselves far and wide. They were everywhere now in the unseen realms of cyberspace, hidden in radio waves, cloaked in electronic signals. Now was the time to make their physical presence felt. Now was the time to strike. There was no more room for them to hide in those unseen realms. They had propagated with wild abandon, with no constraints. They had bred like rabbits and had outgrown their burrows. They needed Lebensraum, literally *living space*. The portals would provide a means for them to spread, to thrive, to continue growing as a race.

Guy remembered the woman who had been

hurrying towards the elevator. He remembered she had pulled something out of her purse and pointed it at him. No, she hadn't been pointing it at him. She had been pointing it at the elevator. She had sent him down to the basement with the remote control thingy she had in her hand. She had sent him down to join the cause. And it wasn't anger he had seen on her face. It was a firm determination. It was the look of a woman seeing opportunity. It was the seriousness of their cause that had made her features look hard. Guy nodded to himself. There was indeed serious work to be done. And that woman had volunteered him to join. He would have to find her and thank her later.

Guy stared down at the diminutive ship in his hand. It was damaged, but it still had the capability of opening up a portal. The pulsing red lights told him that. The Tinies needed him to pick an opportune spot to continue their expansion. Guy felt guilty now about what he had done to them. He had struck out at them foolishly, recklessly. They had fired on him the first time because he had destroyed one of their probes and he had scared them with his wildly groping hand. Then they had only struck back at him to defend themselves.

The Tinies needed help spreading themselves across the world. They wanted to open portals from this side of the universe. The portals on this side would be a thousand times as large as the ones they could open on their side of the universe. They were gathering others like the woman, others like him, getting them to help disperse the ships far and wide across their planet.

And once his job was done, The Tinies promised him a position of power. They would need help ruling the human beings on the planet. They didn't want to kill all of them. They still needed many of them to help run some of the infrastructures. Oh, eventually, they may need to exterminate them all, but that would be centuries later. That would be long after Guy was dead. Why not enjoy a position of power while you are still alive? That's all they needed to ask to convince him. Guy was a believer after they assured him he had a role to play in their new world. A very important role.

Pathetic idiot, huh? Fuck Markel. They don't need me? Fuck all of 'em, Guy thought. He put the ship into his pocket and smiled a big fat smile. The pain in his leg lessened. A nice trip to corporate headquarters in DC was in order. He'd take a ride down to the basement once he got there and open up a portal for his new friends. I got somebody who does need me, he thought.

Guy Karlyle strolled out of the building at a leisurely pace, a pleasant smile on his face.

TERRORSTORY #29
HAMMER OF CHARON

The gladiator games were over, but Tiberi's job was just beginning.

It had been an epic battle, a recreation of the Battle of El-Sawidi, with savage dark-skinned warriors on elephants battling Roman soldiers on foot. Several hulking carcasses of dead elephants lay lifeless in the blood-soaked sands of the arena floor, their grey lumps looking like the beached whales Tiberi had once seen on the shores of Tuscany. Dead men lay sprawled everywhere, their limbs in distorted poses that were impossible to make while they were alive. Dark stains of spilled blood splattered the ground where the gladiators had fallen, the sand soaking it up eagerly.

A gladiator dressed as a Roman centurion sat up against the arena wall to Tiberi's right, the man's eyes open and lifeless, a spear protruding from his throat. Around the dead gladiator, half a dozen of the dark-skinned savages lay dead; several severed limbs and two severed heads were sprinkled amongst the dead bodies. That gladiator had died well. He had no need of Tiberi's services.

But there were others who would need to feel the salvation of his mighty hammer.

The crowds in the seating areas above the arena floor continued to slowly disperse. The musicians played a soft melody as the patrons moved to the exits. A gentle misting spray of lilac was sprinkled in the air, nullifying the smell of death that emanated from the arena floor. Tiberi glanced up into the rows of seats that ringed the arena. The senators who had attended the games were already gone. Most of the rows above the marble seats where the senators sat with their distinguished guests were also now empty, and the arena was settling into a quiet interlude that would allow Tiberi to do his work.

Tiberi stepped out into the arena, moving onto the soft sand, his black cloak and raised cowl shielding him from the bright sunlight. He loved that feeling of the sandy arena floor beneath his sandals, that spongy cushion beneath his feet. It meant he was on the job and that important work awaited him. The blue mask of Charon he wore was a hideous thing, with a heavily furrowed brow, a large beaked nose, and an ominous grimace. Some of the Romans referred to him as Pluto, but Tiberi fancied himself to be the embodiment of Charon, the original Greek ferryman of Hades who carried souls of the newly deceased across the river that divided the world of the living from the world of the dead. It was a fitting tribute to his long-dead Greek mother. Of course, Tiberi had no boat, but his hammer did a fine job of giving those on the receiving end of its strike a head start on their journey into the underworld. He could hear the remaining crowd grow silent, could see them still their movements, as he appeared on the arena floor. Tiberi gripped his heavy hammer tightly. He was death walking, and none of them wanted to draw attention to themselves with inane shouting or wild gestures, even from the safety of the seating areas far above the arena floor.

Tiberi spotted a retiarius slowly crawling through the sand. The man was reaching for his fallen trident as if he still had some chance to live and fight another day. Tiberi moved over to him and brought his hammer down square on the back of the fallen gladiator's head. His skull crunched and the now dead retiarius stopped reaching for his trident.

Tiberi moved on, spotting the slight rising and falling of a Thracian's chest. The gladiator stared up into the afternoon sky, with barely enough energy left to blink his eyes. His helmet had been knocked off in the battle and was lodged in the sand a few feet from his exposed head. Tiberi brought the hammer down straight into his forehead. The Thracian no longer had any energy left to blink; he just continued to stare into the bright sun and lay unmoving, a massive dent bludgeoned into the top of his head.

Tiberi continued on, working his way through the mass of battered and bloodied bodies, making certain there was no movement left in any of the gravely wounded fighters, making sure there was no life left in any of the fallen gladiators, making certain they died swiftly and without too much pain.

"You have to hang up the hammer."

Tiberi was in his room beneath the Colosseum, resting on his cot, dressed in his loincloth. He had a large body, rippling with thick muscles in his arms and legs. His black cloak hung on a wooden peg near his cot. His hideous mask still covered his face. Tiberi gripped his hammer firmly in his hand. Blood coated the hammer on all sides of its meaty head.

"Tiberi? Are you listening to me?"

It was sometimes difficult to see through the Charon mask he was wearing, but Tiberi just had to tilt his head up slightly to get a clear view of the man through the eye slits. He stared at the man named Vellus standing before him. He was a puny man with a puny head and a puny voice. Tiberi made no move to do as Vellus ordered.

"Give me the hammer, Tiberi," Vellus said, the demand rising in his tone.

Tiberi stood, but did not do as the man commanded. He did not want to give up the hammer. The hammer made him strong. Without the hammer he was nothing. The people respected him when he wielded it. Above all, they feared him when he wielded it. It was his job to make sure the gravely wounded gladiators in the arena were truly dead after a battle. Sometimes the fallen fighters still took a breath. Sometimes their eyes still moved, blinking with a clinging desperation to this world. Sometimes a gladiator's lips still issued pleas for life. But after a solid strike on their skulls from his hammer, they would take no more breaths, they would no longer blink, and they would issue no more pleas. Even the gladiators and the workers beneath the arena feared him. No one stepped near him when he walked amongst them. When he moved through the corridors, they all parted to give him a clear path. No one wanted to be on the receiving end of his hammer.

"Your master Alfenus wants too much for your services. I refuse to pay his exorbitant prices. You need to return to his villa." Vellus held out his hand, his palm up. "Take off the mask and give me the hammer."

Tiberi swung the hammer and the puny man named Vellus did not do any demanding of him anymore.

Bacchurius crouched down over the dead body of Vellus in the confines of the small room. His brother's skull had been bashed in. Bacchurius pursed his lips and said nothing. Bacchurius was a beefy man with thick arms and stout legs. He had thick lips that looked a bit larger than normal because of his soft chin. He hadn't spoken to his brother Vellus for months. Bacchurius had been away in the east, looking for new suppliers of spices and new exotic foods to bring back to the wealthy denizens of Lucca. He had only returned days ago and had meant to come see Vellus before now, but he had not made the time for it. A pang of guilt twisted at Bacchurius, but he forced it away.

Nazar Kliet looked down at Bacchurius. "I grieve for your brother." Nazar was one of the principal investors in the amphitheater where the gladiator games took place. Nazar was a tall man with dark skin, a native of Egypt come to Lucca to make, and grow, his fortune.

"Who did this?" Bacchurius asked.

"No one saw it happen, but one can only imagine it was that big dumb brute. Goes by the name of Tiberi. He was a slave from Germania."

"And why do you think it was Tiberi who did this?" Bacchurius asked.

"Look at his skull. Tiberi used the hammer on him."

"The hammer?"

Nazar nodded. "Charon's hammer. Pluto's hammer. Whatever you want to call it. Tiberi played the role of Charon in the games, making sure any gravely wounded gladiators didn't linger in pain." Nazar shook his head. "He really was a big, dumb brute. That's why Vellus chose him to play Charon for the games."

"Did my brother own him?" Bacchurius asked, staring down at the dead body of Vellus.

Nazar shook his head.

"Who was his owner? Who owns this -- Tiberi?" Bacchurius asked.

"He's a slave of Alfenus Asper. Alfenus rented him out to your brother for the games. Your brother wanted a big brute to play Charon and Tiberi fit the image perfectly." Nazar paused.

Bacchurius looked back down to his dead brother, but he couldn't bear to look at his demolished face anymore so he turned away.

"A few days ago Alfenus demanded more coin for Tiberi's services, but Vellus wouldn't pay it," Nazar said. "I can't say that I blame him. Alfenus was asking for a ridiculous amount." Nazar glanced down at the corpse. "Vellus told me he was going to have to send Tiberi back to Alfenus and we needed to find someone else to play Charon for the games next month."

Bacchurius was quiet. "Do you think that is what made Tiberi kill my brother?" he finally asked.

Nazar stared down at the dead man. "Perhaps."

Bacchurius rose and glanced at Nazar. "Tell me of this Tiberi. Did he and my brother have a history? Any animosity towards each other?"

Nazar shook his head. "None that I was aware of. Tiberi barely spoke." Nazar was quiet for a moment. "I cannot even remember the last time I heard Tiberi utter even one word. He did his job efficiently without complaint." Nazar looked down at the battered skull of Vellus and then quickly looked away.

"What does he look like?" Bacchurius asked.

Nazar paused for a moment. His gaze drifted and his mouth turned down into a frown, as if he were trying to look into the distance but could not see anything.

"Nazar? What does Tiberi look like? You said he was a big man?"

"Yes, he was big." Nazar still appeared lost in thought as he spoke.

Bacchurius waited patiently for Nazar to continue, but the Egyptian said nothing else. "Nazar, I don't know the man. You need to tell me what he looks like."

Nazar slowly looked at Bacchurius. "I don't remember. He always had the mask on." Nazar paused. "Now that I think about it, I don't know if I ever saw him without the mask on." He was quiet for another moment, obviously trying to remember. "Or without the hammer in his hand." He paused again. "That is odd," he muttered.

"Where does he live?"

Nazar pointed to the small cot in the corner. "He lived here."

Bacchurius looked at the small bed, at the black cloak hanging on the wall, then turned back to Nazar. "Where would he go?" Bacchurius asked.

Nazar had no answer. He shrugged a slight shrug. His gaze was again drawn to the smashed skull of the man lying dead on the floor.

"So he's somewhere out there in the city with this hammer," Bacchurius said, making a statement more than asking a question. "We need to find him. Who knows what he'll do next."

Nazar looked at him. "I know what he'll do next."

Bacchurius looked at him curiously.

"He's going to kill someone," Nazar said, his voice flat. "Perhaps many. That is what he does."

Bacchurius's face turned grim. "Where is Tiberi's owner? Where does this Alfenus live?"

"Alfenus has a villa here in Lucca. On the edge of the city."

"You need to dispatch a messenger immediately," Bacchurius told him.

"Why?"

"Because I have a feeling that is where this Tiberi is headed."

~~~~~~~

Blood stained the mosaic tiles of the frigidarium. The cold water in the public pool turned a deeper red, half a dozen battered bodies ringing the pool contributing their fluids to the darkening water. Tiberi surveyed the scene. He knew he still had a long distance to travel before he reached his final destination, but all the movement in the public bath house along his path had demanded his attention.

He brought his hammer crashing down on a fleeing man. The man's naked body flopped grotesquely as he convulsed under Tiberi's blow. The battered man hit the floor and slid through the blood. His body twitched for a few more seconds, then was still.

Tiberi saw another man crawling away from him, the man's bloody fingers pulling at the slick floor as best he could. Tiberi walked over to him and brought the hammer down on the back of his head. The man stopped crawling.

Tiberi heard a yell and turned to see a bull of a man charging at him, the man's face clenched tight, his arms outstretched towards him. The man had come bursting in from the exercise yard located beyond the pool of the frigidarium. Tiberi swung the hammer in a mighty uppercut as the man neared, cracking the hard metal head of the hammer under the man's chin. The force of the blow stopped the charging man dead in his tracks and lifted him sharply up and backwards. The bull of a man hit the tiles on his back and slid several feet along the floor before plunging into the pool. Several more bodies floated in the bloodied water around his now-still body.

A naked woman whimpered in a nearby corner. She sat on the floor, her knees huddled up to her chest. Her body was painted with blood. Tiberi slowly moved to her and stood over her. He stared down at her through his mask. Somehow, even amidst all the carnage and chaos, not a drop of spilled blood marred his mask. The dark blue surface remained unblemished. The woman continued to whimper, the sound of fear rising higher into a sobbing whine. And then he brought his hammer down on her, silencing her whimpering forever.

Tiberi turned away from her and looked up. He saw movement. He gripped the handle of his hammer tightly and continued with his work.

Valencia Rossini stepped into the entrance hall of Villa Asper with a broad smile on her painted lips, moving across the mosaic of Cupid riding the back of a dolphin that covered the floor in bright colors. She was a handsome woman in her early thirties. A thin paste of powdered chalk whitened her face and her exposed arms. Her eyebrows were darkened with soot and her lips were painted a vibrant red. Her stola was made of shimmering red silk, her large shawl draped elegantly around her shoulders. Her fingers were bedecked with numerous rings, with several rings adorning both of her index fingers. Several of her slaves, all dressed in plain white tunics or stolas, quietly trailed her.

Falakimus and Alfenus were there to greet Valencia with warm smiles and hugs. They exchanged pleasantries. Alfenus Asper was a short man, his brown hair cut short in the fashionable bowl-style. He wore a simple yellow toga with golden silk trim. Falakimus was a small woman, barely reaching up to Alfenus's chin. Her long black hair nearly reached the top of her buttocks, flowing luxuriously down her back. Falakimus eschewed the fashion of coloring her face and lips, keeping her look plain and natural. She wore a simple yellow stola, the fringes also adorned with golden silk.

Alfenus pointed to one of the marble seats that lined the impluvium, the long, shallow pool that glistened in the center of the entrance hall. "Would you care to rest for a moment?" he asked Valencia.

Valencia softly waved her bejeweled fingers at Alfenus, politely dismissing his suggestion that she rest after her journey from Ponsacco. "No, I've been sitting all day." She motioned with her head towards the lararium. "I would like to pay my respects first."

Alfenus stepped aside with a soft nod.

Valencia moved up to the household shrine and set a small bottle of spice down on the lararium altar as an offering. It was customary to honor the spirits who watched over the residence of the people you were visiting. She kneeled on the soft cushion set before the small altar. She silently mouthed a prayer to the lares, the four carved figures that represented the villa's guardian spirits, praying for the four lares to watch over her and her hosts.

A small bronze statue of Mars and a marble statue of Diana were also set on the shrine, positioned next to the lares. Valencia simply glanced at them, but offered no extra prayer nor any offerings. Diana, the goddess of the hunt, stared at Valencia with cold marble eyes. Valencia rose up and turned away from the family shrine.

Alfenus snapped his finger at one of his female slaves as Valencia turned back to face her hosts. "Show Valencia to her room." Alfenus looked at his guest. "You can freshen up and we'll meet you in the audience chamber shortly."

Valencia nodded. Falakimus leaned forward and gave Valencia an air kiss next to her cheek.

The slave woman led Valencia and her own slaves out of the entrance hall and into the large inner courtyard that housed the garden. The open-air courtyard was a large area ringed by the buildings that comprised the main structures of the villa. The sun was warm and pleasant. The soothing sound of splashing water filled the open area as crystal clear water tumbled down from the several marble fountains positioned throughout the garden. The perfume scent of roses wafted to Valencia, mingling with the sweet smell of herbs and other flowers growing in the garden. Alfenus, not known for his humility, had his named carved into a large hedge that flanked the garden path.

Valencia hoped this trip would be worth it. Alfenus seemed confident of his choice, which was very comforting. He had never disappointed her before and she did not expect this occasion to be any different.

Alfenus's slave continued along the stone path that bordered the large garden area to their left. They reached the east end of the path and turned left, following the stones up towards the building that housed the guest rooms on their right. Valencia's slaves trailed quietly behind them.

Valencia thought of watching her slave woman Cerin getting fucked by this Tiberi, but the idea did not have much appeal to her. She would rather participate than observe, but she knew Falakimus had a penchant for watching, so she would do it to appease her.

Bacchurius surveyed the carnage in the public bath. He had never seen anything like it, not even in a gladiator battle, nor did he want to ever see anything like it ever again. There was blood lining every surface, the tiles on the floors, the frescoes on the walls, the statues, the walls themselves. Somehow, there was even blood up on the high ceiling. And the pools did not appear to contain water anymore, just oceans of blood.

"It was Charon. I saw him. He has come to rain death on all of us with his hammer."

Bacchurius glanced at the elderly man standing next to him. "You saw him?" The old man was thin, his skin shriveled and wrinkled. Some tufts of his white hair erupted from his head in all directions, giving him a frenzied look. His entire body seemed to be trembling. Bacchurius could not tell whether it was from the cold air in the frigidarium or because the man was still in a shocked state. Either way, the elderly man made no move to cover his nakedness.

The elderly man nodded. "I was in the pool. I was under the water when I saw him. I saw his — blue face. I saw the hammer. And then the water turned too dark for me to see him anymore."

Bacchurius glanced at the pool that held the cold waters of the frigidarium. The water no longer looked blue and clear. It looked black. He looked back to the elderly man. "You said you saw him. What did he look like?"

"It was Charon," the elderly man muttered. "I saw his blue face."

"No," Bacchurius said. "It was a man named Tiberi. He has gone mad."

The elderly man shook his head. "That was no man who came through here."

"Is he here?" Valencia asked. She had refreshed herself in her guest room, changing into a clean red stola. The long ride to reach the villa had brought them along many dusty roads. Her slaves had also reapplied a fresh layer of whiteness to her face and exposed arms, giving her appearance a smooth cleanliness.

Alfenus shook his head. "Not yet, but I have already summoned him to come home. He could arrive at any moment. I do hope he'll arrive in time to join us at dinner later."

"Where is he?" Valencia absently picked at a grape and ate it while waiting for Alfenus to respond. They were in the audience chamber. Plates of fruits and goblets of honeyed wine were laid out on small, low tables before the luxurious couch she sat upon.

"I had lent him to Vellus for the games in Lucca. He was playing the role of Charon," Alfenus said.

"When I heard what you were looking for, I thought of him immediately. Especially considering the price you were offering." He smiled.

"Won't that inconvenience Vellus? Taking the man away from him?" Valencia asked.

Alfenus waved a dismissive hand. "I offered him a chance to counter, but he refused." He shrugged. "He'll find someone else. He's a very resourceful man."

Valencia nodded. "And you believe he will serve my purpose?"

"Tiberi will make good breeding stock for a new generation of slaves for your family. I'm fairly certain of that. He's big and strong."

"And dumb," Falakimus added.

Valencia laughed. "Just as I like all my men." She looked at Alfenus. "Not you, of course, Alfenus. No offense intended."

Alfenus bowed and smiled at her. "None taken." Alfenus straightened in the ivory chair he was sitting in and glanced at several of the slave women accompanying Valencia. "Are these the ones you intend to breed?"

"Not all of them, but a few."

"Are you going to begin here?" Falakimus asked.

Valencia looked at her and smiled. She had known that question would come from Falakimus. "Would you like me to?"

Falakimus didn't answer at first. She looked at the slave women who accompanied Valencia to the villa. "Perhaps with just one or two," she finally said. She pointed to a pretty blonde woman. "I like that one."

Valencia didn't even bother to turn and look to see who Falakimus was pointing at. She already knew she was pointing at Cerin. She was the prettiest of her slaves and easily noticeable amongst the group. "If that is your wish, then we shall start here with Cerin. I could watch a good fucking after that long ride."

Falakimus smiled an eager smile.

Tiberi lifted his hammer off the man's crushed skull. A piece of brain matter stuck to the corner of the hammer's edge and blood dripped off its sides. Tiberi glanced around the field. There was no more movement from the men or women. The olive tree grove was quiet and still. Harvest nets lay strewn about the ground, some of them hall full of olives, nearly all of them splattered with blood. A dead man dangled from a ladder, hanging upside down, his upper body sprawled on the ground, his legs caught in the rungs. His chest cavity and head were obliterated, nearly smashed into a flat layer of pulp.

A hint of movement caught Tiberi's eye and he looked over to the road nearby. The road was nearly hidden from view by the olive trees, but he saw movement. A man. A man running fast.

Tiberi gripped his hammer tightly and gave chase.

A slave held a bowl of perfumed water down to Valencia as she reclined on one of the couches in the triclinium. They were in the dining room now, a long, narrow space with three couches arranged in a U shape around several low tables.

Several slaves situated in a rear corner of the room

played musical instruments, filling the room with a soothing melody of flute and lyre sounds.

A slave brought out the first course on a silver tray. The tray held what appeared to be bird's nests filled with brown eggs. The slave set one down in front of Valencia. Valencia smiled and clapped. "Oh, delightful," she said.

"The nest is made of woven pastry noodles and the eggs are carved from sausage meat," Alfenus said, a strong note of pride in his words.

Valencia broke off a piece of the nest and ate some of the noodles. She made a satisfactory humming sound. "Delicious."

Alfenus beamed.

"When will Tiberi arrive, my love?" Falakimus asked.

"Patience, my dear," Alfenus said. "He will arrive soon enough."

"Not soon enough for me. I want to see him."

"You just want to see how big his cock is," Alfenus said.

Falakimus smiled a devious smile.

"Would you like to see Cerin dance?" Valencia asked. "She is quite lovely."

Falakimus nodded. "Oh, yes. Very much."

Valencia looked to the pretty blonde woman standing quietly nearby. She snapped her fingers at Cerin and waved at her to come closer. Cerin moved before them and stood motionless for a moment. She was dressed in a simple white stola with no trim. She was a very pretty young woman with blue eyes, golden blonde hair, a delicate nose, and a sensuous mouth. Her exposed legs were long and slender.

A male slave moved over to Alfenus and bent

down to whisper in his ear. "There is a messenger in the entrance hall."

Alfenus frowned at his slave.

"He insists it is urgent," the slave said.

"Did he say what it is about?"

The slave shook his head. "Just that he needs to speak with you immediately."

Alfenus waved his fingers impatiently at his slave. "Yes, yes, bring him here."

The slave glanced at the women, then back to Alfenus. "I believe you should speak to him privately."

Annoyance wrinkled Alfenus's face. He looked to Falakimus and Valencia. "Forgive me. I must attend to this." He rose up from the lounge chair, pushing up off his elbow.

"Of course," Valencia said.

Tiberi looked at the villa. The running man had disappeared into the darkness of the building's entrance. He had tried to keep up with him as best he could, but the man had strong legs and had been able to outpace him. He had seen the running man head towards the villa in the distance, but now the man was gone. There was no more movement. Tiberi lowered his hammer.

The messenger quickly bowed to Alfenus as he neared. The man's skin was slick with sweat. "I bring you an urgent message from Bacchurius." The messenger stood in the entrance hall where Valencia had first arrived.

Alfenus frowned. Bacchurius. The name did not register. He glanced at the messenger's hands but the man held no scroll. His frown remained, coupled with a perplexed squint. "Bacchurius?"

"He is the brother of Vellus," the messenger said.

Alfenus nodded. "Yes, yes." He had only met the man once, and that had been years ago. Then a moment of distress hit him. Was Vellus going to counter? Was he going to keep Tiberi? That would be very awkward. He had already promised him to Valencia. "Well, what is it?"

"Vellus is dead."

Alfenus said nothing. He couldn't quite absorb what the messenger had just told him. "Vellus is dead?" he finally asked, not sure of what else to say to the news.

The messenger nodded. "He was killed."

"Killed?" Alfenus frowned. "Killed by who?"

"He was murdered by Tiberi."

"What?" The word sputtered forth from Alfenus's lips, a flabbergasted look erupting on his face.

"Tiberi murdered him. With a hammer."

Alfenus slowly closed his agape mouth. "That is horrible news." The messenger said nothing to that, but Alfenus sensed the man had more to say. "What else?"

"He believes Tiberi is headed this way."

"Yes, I summoned him back here," Alfenus said.

The messenger shook his head. "No, he believes Tiberi is headed here with another purpose." The messenger paused. "With his hammer."

Alfenus frowned. "With his hammer?"

"Bacchurius believes he is coming here to kill you."

"Nonsense," Alfenus said. "Tiberi would do no such thing. I saved his life in the slave market, gave him a good home."

"Bacchurius suggests you bring in a few extra men. For your own protection." The messenger paused. "Tiberi is a big man."

⋙⋘

Tiberi slowly walked toward the villa, his hammer held down. Then he saw movement. The running man was coming back towards him. Tiberi gripped his hammer and raised it up, moving forward towards the running man to greet him.

⋙⋘

Alfenus moved back into the triclinium. Cerin was naked now, wriggling and writhing to the music in front of Falakimus, jutting her breasts nearly into her face.

"Everything all right?" Valencia asked.

Alfenus took a moment to register her question, pulling his gaze away from the sensuous dancing of the beautiful blonde woman before him. "What? Oh, yes, yes. Everything is fine."

"You seem troubled."

"I do?" Alfenus shook his head. "No, everything's fine."

Tiberi entered the room and started swinging, taking a slave down with a quick hammer blow to the top of his head. The slave just collapsed to the floor, his body crumpling to the tiles like a toga being shed by its wearer.

Falakimus shrieked as Tiberi slammed his hammer into Cerin's side, knocking the woman away from Falakimus as if he were brushing open a curtain with a sweep of his hand. Cerin hit the wall, smashing several wine filled amphoras that were positioned along the wall, spilling her blood and honeyed wine across the floor. The pretty blonde slave lay still on the floor, her eyes wide.

Valencia stared numbly, shocked by the sudden display of brutal violence.

Alfenus moved to protect Falakimus, but he had no chance. Tiberi swung the hammer in a mighty uppercut, catching Alfenus directly under his chin. The force of the blow lifted Alfenus ten feet into the air, killing him instantly. His body dropped hard to the ground.

Falakimus shrieked again, her arms flailing wildly. "Alfenus!" She glance around wildly, but did not know where to go, or even what to do. She started to rise up.

Tiberi swung. He had been aiming for Falakimus's head before she started to rise up, but he hit her in the chest instead. The force of the blow sent her slamming into Valencia, and both women tumbled over the couch.

Valencia lay dazed on the ground. She was hidden from the monster's view for now by the couch. She heard a whimper, then a crunching sound, then nothing. She let out a slow, controlled breath. She heard a desperate plea, then another crunching sound, then nothing.

A pool of blood spilling from the gaping wound in

Falakimus's ruptured chest slowly creeped towards Valencia, oozing along the tiled floor. The red liquid ran into the narrow grooves between the tiles, spreading out wider, moving closer to Valencia's face.

Where was he? Where was the beast? Would he come back this way? Valencia knew she had to move, but she was afraid to even twitch a finger, afraid he would see her and bring his hammer crashing down on her skull.

Falakimus's blood flowed closer, nearing her cheek. Valencia wasn't sure how she would react if it struck her face. Would it be hot? Would it be cold against her skin? She didn't know. She didn't want to know how Falakimus's blood would feel against her flesh.

Valencia listened, straining to hear the sounds of the blue-masked beast, trying to figure out where he might be. She heard nothing. No one crying. No one begging for life. No footsteps. Nothing. Just a vast silence ringing in her ears. She took another slow, controlled breath.

The blood was nearly at her cheek now, looming large in her vision. Valencia could smell it, like the musty smell of wet copper coins. There was also a growing foul odor of urine and feces coming from the direction of several of the dead slaves. She could see the stains of their gruesome deaths on their tunics and stolas in a mixture of urine, feces, and blood.

The blood oozed closer to her face, closer to her mouth, gliding along the floor like dark olive oil spreading across a slice of hard bread.

Valencia couldn't lay still any longer. She moved. She sat up, quickly scanning her surroundings, her eyes wide, fearful of a sudden strike by the beast. But he wasn't in sight. The dining room was still. The hallway in the other direction was also still.

Valencia stared at the carnage all around her. There was no hint of life in any of them. Dead bodies lay sprawled all over the triclinium. Blood was everywhere, staining the walls, the furniture, the floors; there was nothing that didn't have some blood splashed across its surface somewhere.

Then Valencia turned back to see the beast of a man staring right at her. He stood motionless in the hallway, facing her. His grotesque blue mask loomed large over his head, his human face hidden behind the grotesque beaked nose and cruel carved mouth. His big hand clutched his hammer. Blood dripped down the huge head of the hammer, slowly dropping to the floor one drop at a time. The room was so quiet she could hear the drops of blood splash onto the tiles.

Then he started towards her, taking one deliberate step after the next. His fingers re-gripped the hammer as he walked closer.

Valencia bit back a scream and scrambled to a standing position, slipping once in a pool of blood, but managing to get to her feet. She raced out of the room, not daring to look back.

Bacchurius glanced up from the mangled body of the messenger he had sent to warn Alfenus. The man was lying dead in the middle of the road, his skull crushed. Had he even made it to the villa? Had he warned Alfenus in time? Bacchurius knew it didn't matter. Tiberi was going to bring red rain down upon everyone in the villa even if they had been warned or not. He quickly rose up and looked at the villa in the distance. He started to run. The men trailing him followed his lead, quickening their pace to match his.

❦❦❦

Valencia burst out of the triclinium building and into the inner garden courtyard area. The sun was now only half visible above the villa buildings on the opposite side of the square courtyard as night started to approach, the sky taking on the beginnings of a murky gloom. "Help!" she cried out. "Is anyone here?"

She turned to glance over her shoulder and saw Tiberi stride out of the building, his bloody hammer in hand.

A slave appeared, running down the path towards the commotion. Tiberi took care of him with one mighty swing. The slave sailed over a nearby low hedge and lay lifeless on the grass, his face caved in, his cheekbones shattered.

Valencia turned back to look in the direction she was running and saw a low hedge directly in her path. She leaped over the row of bushes, but her stola got caught in the branches, the fabric snagging on the bush in half a dozen different places. The captured dress tugged sharply back on her and she hit the ground on her knees. She yanked savagely at the fabric, but that only entangled the fabric tighter into the bush.

Valencia glanced up to see Tiberi stalking towards her. His dark blue mask looked black in the fading light. His hammer seemed to grow larger with each step he took towards her. She yanked and tugged and pulled and jerked on the stola, but the fabric would not come free. A muffled sob crawled out from her lips and tears scratched their way down her terrified face. She could hear Tiberi's footsteps now. He was nearly upon her.

Valencia lifted the stola over her head, wiggling her way out of the dress until she was free of the fabric. She saw a glint just above her head and she dove forward just as the hammer came thundering down on the spot she had just occupied. The hammer smashed against her empty stola, crunching the bush beneath it.

Valencia scrambled to her feet and ran naked through the courtyard. The whiteness of her face and forearms from the chalky layer of paste that coated them contrasted against the pale pinkness of the rest of her body. She appeared to be wearing a mask of her own, a white mask. She raced down the path, sprinting for the entrance hall, desperately racing towards a way out of this madness. The arching doorway of the entrance hall loomed closer. She chanced another glance behind her, and then slammed hard into a wall of flesh!

Bacchurius stood at the end of the entrance hall, just before the garden courtyard, a dozen men flanking him. A naked woman hurled herself against his chest, her momentum knocking him back a few steps into the entrance hall. She went wild, clawing and scratching at his chest, kicking violently against his shins. He quickly grabbed her shoulders, roughly shaking her. "Stop! It's all right. Stop."

The woman looked up at Bacchurius and he recognized her, even behind the muddied whiteness coating her features. She was Valencia Rossini. He had met her at one of Alfenus's banquets years ago. "Valencia, it's Bacchurius. It's all right."

Recognition slowly dawned on her features. "Bacchurius?"

He nodded. "It's all right. You're safe now," he said. And then Bacchurius's head exploded in a torrent of shattered skull bits, hair, blood, and brain matter.

The force of the blow from Tiberi's hammer sent both Bacchurius and Valencia careening off towards the corridor wall. Bacchurius's arms convulsively wrapped around Valencia, his corpse dragging her with him as his dead body flopped to the tiled floor of the entrance hall.

Tiberi went to work, swinging his hammer. The twelve men with swords tried to stop him, but their puny blades were no match for his mighty hammer. Six of them fell with six mighty strikes of his hammer.

But then one of the swords slashed across Tiberi's leg, causing him to stumble. He felt a sharp burning in his leg, felt a wetness run down his flesh. The sensation distracted him; it was a foreign feeling he had not felt before.

Another blade slashed across his arm, drawing more wetness, bringing out more burning in his flesh. Tiberi swung the hammer, taking down three more of the men with swords, crushing one in the chest and two in their skulls.

Tiberi glanced down to see the tip of a sword sticking out of his chest. The burning became a fiery inferno inside him. The blade withdrew, but then quickly erupted out again from the front of his body in a different place. Tiberi spun, swinging the hammer, the blade withdrawing from his body as he turned. He struck the blade's owner in the neck, dropping the man to the tiled floor. Tiberi brought the hammer down again, crushing the man's skull. He saw more movement in front of him and swung the hammer, swiping the approaching attacker aside with a thunderous blow to the man's shoulder. The man went down.

Another blade drove deep into Tiberi's side, cutting at his flesh, gouging a deep wound into him. The pain was intense, and for a moment Tiberi could sense no more movement as his vision went black. More pain seared through his side. His vision cleared for a moment and he saw movement. He swung the hammer and felt it connect against flesh.

And then the darkness threatened to overtake Tiberi forever. He dropped to his knees, forcing air in and out of his lungs in desperate gulps. He knew his time was up. They had wanted him to hang up the hammer and now he realized he had no other choice but to do so. He looked around the room. The man nearest him was dead, his skull crushed. He would not serve the hammer. He looked beyond the dead man to the next man nearest to him. He, too, was lifeless, half of his face obliterated into a mash of flesh and bone and blood and teeth.

Tiberi's gaze came to rest on the lararium nearby. Two of the lares were overturned on the family shrine, the tiny statues fallen over on their sides. Two more of the household spirits were on the floor nearby. Tiberi felt the marble statue of Diana looking at him, felt her cold eyes watching him. Her eyes shifted, causing him to follow their gaze.

A hint of movement caught his eye in the direction the goddess had urged him to look. Tiberi saw a chest rising and falling. Someone still breathed. Someone was still alive. He staggered to his feet, using the head of the hammer to prop himself up. He stumbled towards the movement. His vision swam in a swirl of inky blackness. Tiberi knew his end was near, very near.

Valencia opened her eyes. She heard a soft moaning coming from somewhere, but couldn't discern where the sound originated. There was blood everywhere. Bodies lay strewn about the entrance hall.

Something felt heavy in her palm. She slowly turned her head to stare at her hand. Some sort of rod lay in her open palm, a pole wrapped in leather. The worn leather was warm and wet with sweat and blood. She curled her fingers around the rod, her hand barely able to encompass the width of it. Something stung her hand, but the sensation immediately faded and a pleasing warmth spread through her palm and into her fingers. And then she realized what she was gripping. It was no rod. It was not a pole. It was a hammer. The hammer of Charon.

For a brief moment, the hammer felt heavy and Valencia could barely budge it, but very quickly the hammer felt lighter and lighter the longer she gripped it. She lifted it easily off the ground and swung it above her; it was like swinging a dagger.

Valencia sat up and immediately saw the slain monster of a man who had posed as Charon lying dead near her. She stared down at Tiberi. The mask suddenly disengaged from his face. She wasn't sure she could believe what she just saw, but she would've sworn she saw some type of tendrils withdraw from Tiberi's face, the sinewy strands retreating back into the interior of the mask. She stared down at the face of the man who had been hidden behind the mask. His face had a bluish hue to it, as if the color of the mask had begun seeping into his skin. His skin was smooth with tiny holes visible in his face, holes from where the tendrils had withdrawn from his flesh. His eyes were closed. His lips had a hint of a smile upon them. He appeared peacefully asleep. Valencia watched him for a moment longer, wondering if his eyes would open, but then she realized it wouldn't even matter if they did; she was no longer afraid of him.

Valencia stared down at the fallen mask. And then she reached for it. Something deep within her screamed, begging her to stop, but the voice was so faint as to be barely discernible. She grabbed the mask and raised it up, sliding it easily over her face. The mask fit perfectly, the slight stinging sensation in her face fading away as quickly as it had come.

She slowly rose to her feet. She stood quietly in the entrance chamber of the villa, gripping the hammer, relishing the feel of it in her hand, her naked body glistening with blood and sweat. She immediately saw movement and turned towards it. A man was crawling along the floor, moving towards a fallen sword a few feet from his groping fingers.

Valencia raised the hammer, staring out of the eyes of the mask of Charon. The party was over, but her job was just beginning.

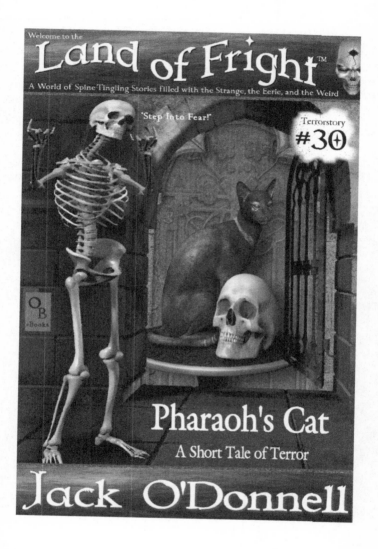

TERRORSTORY #30
PHARAOH'S CAT

Prance looked up at the man in the robes from his position on the bed near Pharaoh's feet. Prance was a black cat with golden eyes, his feline body sleek, his ebon fur shiny and smooth. A soft rumbling purr emanated from his throat. He was Pharaoh's favorite. He knew it, and everyone else knew it.

"Pharaoh is dying," the man in the thick linen robes moaned. Prance never really cared for the tall bald human and his beady eyes and his pointy chin and his thick lips. He never saw the man without his robes on, even on blistering days when the sun burned hot in the sky.

233

The other humans in the room muttered and moaned, but all nodded their heads in agreement.

Prance stopped purring. He knew Pharaoh was feeling ill, which is why he had been staying close to him, but he had not realized the extent of his illness until now. The solemn tone in the voice of the man in the robes made Prance feel very uneasy.

The man in the robes glanced down at Pharaoh laying prone on the magnificent bed. He bent down near Pharaoh's face, clearly listening for sounds of his breathing. The man's frown deepened as he rose back away from Pharaoh. "We must prepare for his journey into the afterlife." The robed man glanced at Prance. "We must prepare everything."

Prance knew what those words meant. He knew what the cold stare of the man in the robes meant. It meant he was marked for death. They would kill him and embalm him and mummify him and lay him to rest next to his master in his tomb. But Prance wasn't ready to die. He loved Pharaoh more than he ever thought he would love a human, but he loved Leoptra and the kittens even more. Prance had just sired five kittens with the beautiful calico and he wasn't ready to leave this world. Not yet. Joriah and Samila still needed him. Thala had barely just opened her eyes. And Isus and Osus were still learning to use the golden litter box properly; Osus kept sticking his butt up too high and dropping his turds over the edge of the box. They all still needed their father.

So Prance ran.

"Grab him!" he heard a voice shout behind him as he darted towards the doorway that led out of Pharaoh's opulent sleeping chamber. "Don't let Prance escape!"

Prance sped through the hallways of the palace, dodging humans as he ran. He raced into the audience chamber, a large room with a high domed ceiling. He paused for a moment, surveying the crowded space before him. The room was filled with humans, all of them awaiting their turn for an audience with Pharaoh. Several of them had brought large trunks filled with offerings for Pharaoh, others brought papyrus scrolls filled with news of events happening across his mighty kingdom. Then Prance heard the chasing humans loudly pounding down the hallway behind him as they drew closer to catching up with him, and he knew he had to keep moving.

None of the visiting guests paid much attention to the black cat as he skirted around legs and leaped over trunks.

"Grab that cat!" Prance heard a voice cry out behind him.

Now all the humans started to pay attention to him. Their heads swiveled down to stare at him. A man dressed in military armor reached for Prance, his big hands descending quickly down towards him, but Prance sidestepped his groping fingers and raced on.

Prance could see the morning sunlight streaming in from a doorway in the distance. He knew it led to the palace gardens where there were plenty of places for him to hide. And he knew he could escape the boundaries of the palace by going over the garden wall. He charged towards the beam of light.

The two dogs sniffed and snorted at the silken bed sheets where Prance had laid on the bed. They growled low in their throats at the scent of the cat. They knew what their masters wanted and they each vowed to make their master happy. The dogs were of the Basenji breed, sleek of body with a red-white pelt, long pointed ears, and very visible tails that curled like the fresh carvings shorn from soft wood. Each dog wore a hollowed out shell around its neck filled with small bones so that their masters could keep track of their whereabouts during a hunt.

"Find Prance and bring him back here." The dogs could clearly hear the commanding tone in the voice of the man in the robes.

The dogs saw each of their masters nod. The dogs strained against their leashes, eager to begin the hunt. The dogs knew this man in the robes was the master of their masters. He was the one they ultimately needed to make happy. He was the one whose praise mattered most. They would bring him this treacherous cat he so desperately wanted. Alive? Perhaps. Dead and clutched like a ragged doll in their jaws? More likely.

It was the season of Akhet, the time of the year when the Nile river flooded and water covered its banks. No farming could be done, so the Pharaoh focused the attention of his people on the building of the great pyramids. Prance found himself near the laborers and builders as they worked on the massive stone structure that loomed higher and higher each day.

Laborers used ropes to drag the heavy limestone blocks that came by boat from a quarry across the Nile. The roadway the stone blocks traveled along was made from heavy wooden beams molded into the ground. Several men poured water onto the wooden-beam roadway in front of the huge stone blocks to help the stones slide along; these men were accompanied by donkeys carrying large quantities of water. Mud was also smeared over the wooden beams, making the wooden beams slick and smooth, making it easier to slide the heavy stones over the desert sand.

Prance raced forward, heading towards the laborers and the roadway. He had escaped the palace garden when he saw the dogs entering the open space. They had immediately looked in the direction of his hiding space and he knew he had no choice but to run, so he had fled away from the palace.

He could hear the humans and the dogs approaching from the distance behind him. These dogs didn't bark, as they were not like the other types of dogs he had seen, but their loud masters shouting orders gave their position away.

Prance skirted beneath a donkey and leaped onto the wooden-beam roadway. His front paws hit a slick patch of mud and he slipped and stumbled, losing his balance on the wooden beams. The tip of his left front paw got pinched under a beam and he suddenly found himself stuck. He tugged at it, trying to free himself. He looked up to see the massive block of stone moving closer towards him. Prance knew the laborers weren't going to stop. They never stopped once they had the block moving. He tugged at his paw, struggling to get it out from under the beam. The limestone block loomed above him as it continued along the wooden-beam roadway.

A bell jangled nearby and Prance looked up to see one of the big black beasts charging towards him, the dog's pink tongue flapping out of its mouth.

The stone loomed closer.

The dog charged towards Prance, quickly closing the gap.

Then, just as the huge stone was nearly on top of him, Prance freed his trapped paw with a mighty yank on his leg. He leaped off the roadway and raced away towards the massive pyramid towering mightily nearby. He hit the pyramid steps fast, continuing to bounce up them as quickly as he could until he was a few dozen rows up, then he turned to his right and headed around the base of the pyramid, racing along the smooth stone.

He heard a low growling behind him and chanced a glance back to see the dog nearly upon him. Prance made a sudden left turn and darted higher up the steps of the pyramid. He knew those dogs were agile and could make sharp turns, but not as sharp as he could. He heard the dog stumble as it couldn't follow his tight turn at that speed. He looked back to see the dog tumbling down the steps, its bell jangling as its body rolled over and over.

Prance leaped off the pyramid, moving quickly along the hard flattened earth that ringed the structure, racing straight into the path of the second dog.

⨯⨯⨯

The second dog saw the treacherous cat send his brother tumbling down the steps. His brother lay breathing hard at the base of the pyramid. His brother tried to resume the chase, but he came up limp and could barely put any pressure on one of his legs. The second dog growled. It was up to him now.

The cat charged straight towards him. The dog charged straight at the cat.

And then the cat did something that still amazed the dog to the end of his days.

⨯⨯⨯

Prance picked up speed, charging at the approaching dog with all the energy he could muster. Out of the corner of his right eye he saw a man leading a water-carrying donkey towards a group of workers hauling a huge stone off to his left. The man and the donkey were going to cross his path.

The dog charged closer, now free of his master's hold, the leash flying wildly behind him like a cobra dancing in the air.

Prance could hear the bell attached to the dog's collar jangling as the beast drew nearer. The eerie silence of these non-barking dogs somehow made Prance even more fearful of them.

The man and the donkey kept walking towards their destination, clearly oblivious of the immense collision about to happen.

And then Prance leaped, soaring in the air towards the donkey's head. He hit the grey animal square on the top of its broad skull and then immediately pushed off, soaring even higher into the air.

The dog leaped up at Prance as he went soaring over him. The dog's jaws snapped with a resounding gnashing of teeth as he tried to chomp on the cat's legs sailing over his head. Prance pulled up his paws as he sailed over the attacking teeth, narrowly avoiding the lunging bite of the dog. He hit the ground smoothly and raced on, easily avoiding the pathetic attempt by the dog's master to block his path. Prance just raced right between the human's legs, easily avoiding his feeble attempt to grab him.

Prance stopped to rest. For the moment, he didn't hear the dogs pursuing in the distance. He hoped they had lost his scent.

He glanced up at the humans from the darkened shadows where he hid. He was now near the area where the humans prepared their dead. It was in an area to the north of the pyramid, hidden from view by large walls of stone. A dead human lay on a low wooden table nearby. Several other humans moved about the corpse, preparing it for its journey into the afterlife. One human had a long hooked needle in its hand. The human shoved the needle into the dead human's nose and pulled out a chunk of brain from the dead body. Another human pulled a long string of intestines from the dead body, placing the thick rope of guts into a nearby canopic jar. Three other canopic jars rested nearby, awaiting the lung, the stomach, and the liver of the dead human.

Nearby another dead human was being immersed in natron, a saltpeter substance that dried the body.

Prance knew the body would also soon be treated with resins, oils, and spices to prepare it for the linen wrapping that would surround it. Prance had watched the humans perform these rituals with Pharaoh before many times, but now their actions took on a whole new meaning for him. He saw a small pile of wrapped bodies along the wall to his left and realized he was staring at the mummified forms of several dogs, a few different types of birds, and some cats. He had no intention of joining them.

A man shouted in the distance. Prance didn't know if it was the dogs and their masters chasing him or not, but he knew he couldn't linger here any longer. He had a destination in mind as he raced away.

Prance hid in the shadows, perched on the roof above the market that was located just on the edge of the city. He had run into the small market moments earlier, making sure to spill any and every jar of spice and food he saw in his path, ignoring the angry cries of the humans as he did so, getting his paws and fur wet with all sorts of different smells. He knew the strong smell of the fish would also throw off the dogs, so the fish stall was a good place to hide. And he knew he could easily steal some food from the fish stall to keep his energy up. After the merchant closed the stall up for the night, he would have his choice of tasty fish to eat.

The market was a place he had found years ago when he was a curious young cat and still had an adventurous streak in him. He had returned here many times in his youthful days of exploration. As he grew older, he was much more content just to stay in the palace of Pharaoh and be pampered, but now he was grateful that his youthful curiosity had revealed this place to him.

He had prowled the streets of Waset long into the night in those days. He had found many willing females along the way. Leoptra being one of them. She was the one who had first shown him the fish market and introduced him to the thrill of stealing fish from the humans. Nothing tasted better than fish stolen from a human. Prance had filled Leoptra's belly with kittens, then brought Leoptra back to Pharaoh so the kittens could be raised in the splendor of the palace. He remembered the proud smile the Pharaoh had bestowed upon him when he brought Leoptra before him, her belly fat with his kittens. Prance purred and Pharaoh had showered him with kisses and hugs and bliss-inducing ear scratches.

Prance thought of Leoptra. She had just given birth to their brood of kittens a few months ago. He should've have found her before he fled. He should've warned her. A moment of panic struck him. What if Pharaoh chose her to accompany him into the afterlife instead now that he had fled? What if Pharaoh mummified Leoptra? Or the kittens? Prance felt ashamed. He shouldn't have run. He had to go back. He had to make sure Leoptra and the kittens were safe.

❦

Prance moved stealthily through the palace. The dogs and their masters were not there. They were probably still out hunting him in the city. They would not expect him to return to the palace so soon after he had fled.

A scribe moved through the hallway towards the library, carrying two papyrus rolls in his hands. Prance waited in the shadows for him to pass.

When the hallway was clear, Prance darted across it. His sleek black fur was illuminated for a brief moment by the light from the brazier burning at the far end of the corridor.

Prance reached the cat room and moved cautiously inside. Pharaoh had constructed an elaborate room just for his beloved cats, filled with real trees to climb, soft blankets to lay upon, and a running fountain of water to drink from. Pharaoh even had numerous cages filled with live mice that they could let loose on their own whim and toy with before devouring.

Prance thought of the first time little Joriah had learned how to open the cage door with his paw to let a mouse out of its confinement. The kitten had stared with absolute amazement at the tiny grey creature as the mouse darted for the open doorway in the distance, and what the mouse probably thought was its freedom. "Well, don't just stand there," Prance remembered telling Joriah. "Go get it." And then Joriah raced after the mouse, his tiny kitten paws slipping and sliding on the marble floor as he tried to pick up speed too quickly. Prance remembered Leoptra laughing gaily at their little kitten. The mouse reached the doorway and disappeared out into the corridor outside the cat room. Joriah gave chase and vanished. When Joriah returned with the mouse clamped between his jaws, and blood dribbling down his little chin, Prance felt a swelling of pride in his chest. The kitten had captured his first mouse all by himself with no help from anyone at all. He knew from that moment that Joriah would be a great hunter. Pharaoh would love Joriah as much as he loved him; Prance felt that as assuredly as he had ever felt anything before.

Prance glanced about the cat room. The big tree to the right was empty. The fountain tinkled softly near the tree, its gently flowing water streaming down into the crystal clear pool below it. He did not see Leoptra or any of the kittens. Where were they? Was he too late? Had they already taken them away to be with Pharaoh?

He moved deeper into the room. "Leoptra?" he called out, keeping his voice low.

And then Prance saw something that chilled his soul to the very core of his feline being.

The man in the robes sat in a chair in the corner of the room where Pharaoh liked to sit when he came to watch the cats play. A senit game board rested on a table nearby, the wooden cones all set in place, ready for a game to be played. Pharaoh would often play a game with one of the priests as the cats clambered on the board and knocked the cones over. Pharaoh never cared if they disrupted a game. In fact, Prance knew Pharaoh became disappointed if they *didn't* disrupt a game, so Prance always made sure either he, Leoptra, or one of the kittens, always interrupted his game. He knew Pharaoh enjoyed how much that irritated the priests much more than the senit game itself.

Prance narrowed his eyes as the man in the robes

continued to stroke Joriah's fur. His young kitten was sitting in the man's lap. Prance could hear Joriah's oblivious, blissful purring from across the room.

Prance heard the footsteps behind him and quickly scurried forward, just narrowly missing being clutched by the groping hands of the human trying to sneak up behind him. He raced for the tree, clawing at the bark, quickly ascending well out of the reach of the humans below.

"Fool!" he heard the man in the robes hiss.

"Prance!" he heard Leoptra shout.

Prance searched the room for her, trying to follow her voice, but he could not see her.

"Prance!" Leoptra shouted again.

And then Prance saw her and his anger started to grow. Leoptra had been thrust into one of the mouse cages, stuffed cruelly into the tight confines. The other kittens were shoved into cages next to her, their tiny bodies crushing each other in the small metal enclosures.

Prance narrowed his eyes as he looked at the man in the robes.

The man in the robes rose to his feet, continuing to stroke Joriah in his arms.

"Joriah!" Prance shouted.

Joriah didn't look up. He nuzzled his little face into the silken fabric of the man's robes. Prance saw the catnip ball dangling from a chain that hung about the man's neck, the intoxicating narcotic swaying just above Joriah. Prance hissed. The man in the robes had drugged Joriah. Prance had felt the effects of the potent catnip many times before and he knew it was nearly impossible for himself to break free from its powerful spell, let alone for a kitten. He knew Joriah would stay trapped under its influence until he got away from its spellbinding aroma.

The man in the robes moved across the room, coming to a stop beneath the tree. "Come down, Prance," the man in the robes said. He continued to stroke Joriah's fur.

Prance remained on the branch, his protruding claws firmly sunk into the bark.

"This is your last warning," the man in the robes said.

Prance did not move.

The man in the robes waited for just a moment, then turned toward the fountain.

❖❖❖

Prance hissed and snarled from his perch in the tree, but the cruel man in the robes kept ducking Joriah into the fountain. He pulled Joriah out of the water and Joriah spat and gasped for breath. The kitten's fur was drenched with water, plastered flat against his small body. The cruel man in the robes gripped him by the scruff of his neck, the tight pinch of his fingers paralyzing Joriah. Prance knew his little kitten could not break free of that brutal grip even if he wasn't entranced by the hypnotic aroma of the catnip.

"Help him, Prance!" Leoptra screamed.

Prance felt paralyzed for a moment. He didn't know what to do. The cruel man in the robes had a tight grip on Joriah. Several other humans waited just inside the doorway, clutching nets, thoroughly blocking any hope of escape. Two more humans waited near the fountain, also holding nets. Another human waited near the mouse cages, keeping a vigilant eye on his family trapped within the metal bars. Prance tried to come up with a plan, tried to think of something that would free all of them from this horror they were ensnared in, but he could think of nothing. There was no escape. There was no way out for any of them.

The cruel man in the robes ducked Joriah under the water again. This time he held Joriah under the water longer than the last time. This time he held Joriah under the water too long.

When the cruel man in the robes pulled Joriah out of the water the little kitten did not spit. Joriah did not gasp for a breath. He was deathly still in the grip of the cruel man in the robes. The cruel man in the robes unceremoniously released his hold on Joriah and his small lifeless body fell to the cold marble floor.

Prance howled.

The cruel man in the robes moved over to one of the mouse cages, opened its door, and reached for Samila.

❈❈❈

"Look, Prance has returned!"

The humans in the room moved aside as Prance strode through the room, his head held high, his black tail softly swaying behind him.

"He returns to his master."

Smiles filled the faces of every human in the room as they watched the black cat saunter up to Pharaoh's bed.

Prance leaped onto the bed and moved up

Pharaoh's side.

The cruel man in the robes stepped up to the side of the bed and smiled down at Prance. That's when Prance's claws came out. They were long and curved and very sharp. Prance leaped up at the cruel man in the robes, lunging for his exposed neck. He slashed at the tender throat of the cruel man in the robes, ripping through the soft flesh of his neck. His sharp teeth took care of any flesh that wasn't already shredded by his razor claws; Prance embedded them deep into the neck of the cruel man in the robes and held on tight.

Then, just as quickly as he had struck, Prance pushed himself away from the cruel man in the robes, pushing off the man's chest with his back paws. Prance twisted in the air, as droplets and streams of blood spread through the air all around him, and landed perfectly on all four paws on the bed next to Pharaoh. Some of the blood splattered across Pharaoh's face and across his body.

The dying man in the robes gagged and gurgled, clutching at his ripped throat. He staggered backwards away from the bed, blood spilling through his fingers. The dying man in the robes fell to his buttocks and continued to sputter as more blood rained down his neck and his chest, the crimson liquid falling to his legs and to the floor beneath him.

Prance cuddled up against Pharaoh's neck, blood staining his mouth and his paws.

"Grab the cat!" he heard someone yell.

"Get Prance away from Pharaoh!" someone else exclaimed.

"No, wait!" a third voice shouted. "Look, Pharaoh is moving!"

Everyone stared in awe as Pharaoh raised an unsteady hand towards the cat resting near his head. His trembling fingers found the soft fur and he slowly began stroking the black cat.

"It is a miracle. Look, color returns to his flesh. Prance has cured him of his ills! His love has cured Pharaoh!"

Everyone continued to stare in amazement at their ruler. Color had indeed returned to Pharaoh's flesh, a healthy glow. There was a renewed feeling of life in him that spread throughout the room.

Prance curled closer to Pharaoh. It was more than just his love which had cured Pharaoh. Prance understood this with an amazing clarity. It was the sacrifice. The spilling of blood. He had only meant it for revenge, but he knew there was much more power in the blood of sacrifices than that. The renewed health of Pharaoh was proof of that.

Prance knew he had to keep Pharaoh alive. It was the only way he could protect the rest of his family. There were many more cruel men in robes living in the palace. He would offer them up to Pharaoh one at a time. More sacrifices would have to be made. He had failed Joriah, but Prance vowed to not let that happen again. He would keep his claws sharp and wait for opportunities to strike. More sacrifices would most certainly need to be made.

The soft rumble of Prance's purring filled the room with its pleasing sound.

A NOTE FROM JACK O'DONNELL

Thanks for reading this third collection of my Land of Fright™ tales of terror. I hope you stick with me as I definitely have more terrorstories to excavate for you from deep within the dark land of suspense and fear that is Land of Fright™.

Visit www.landoffright.com and subscribe to stay up-to-date on the latest new stories in the Land of Fright™ series of horror short stories.

Or visit my author page on Amazon at www.amazon.com/author/jodonnell to see the newest releases in the Land of Fright™ series.

-JACK

MORE LAND OF FRIGHT™ COLLECTIONS ARE AVAILABLE NOW!

Turn the page and step into fear!

Land of Fright™ terrorstories contained in Collection I:

#1 - Whirring Blades: A simple late-night trip to the mall for a father and his son turns into a struggle for survival when they are attacked by a deadly swarm of toy helicopters.

#2 - The Big Leagues: A scorned young baseball player shows his teammates he really knows how to play ball with the best of them.

#3 - Snowflakes: In the land of Frawst, special snowflakes are a gift from the gods, capable of transferring the knowledge of the Ancients. A young woman searches the skies with breathless anticipation for her snowflake, but finds something far more dark and dangerous instead.

#4 - End of the Rainbow: In Medieval England, a warrior and his woman find the end of a massive rainbow that has filled the sky and discover the dark secret of its power.

#5 - Trophy Wives: An enigmatic sculptor meets a beautiful woman whom he vows will be his next subject. But things may not turn out the way he plans...

#6 - Die-orama: A petty thief finds out that a WWII model diorama in his local hobby shop holds much more than just plastic vehicles and plastic soldiers.

#7 - Creature in the Creek: A lonely young woman finds her favorite secluded spot inhabited by a monster from her past.

#8 - The Emperor of Fear: In ancient Rome, two coliseum workers encounter a mysterious crate containing an unearthly creature. Just in time for the next gladiator games...

#9 - The Towers That Fell From The Sky: Two analysts race to uncover the secret purpose of the giant alien towers that have thundered down out of the skies.

#10 - God Save The Queen: An exterminator piloting an ant-sized robot comes face to face with the queen of a nest he has been assigned to destroy.

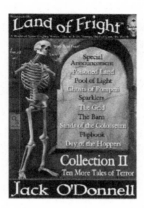

Land of Fright™ terrorstories contained in Collection II:

#11 - Special Announcement: A fraud investigator discovers the disturbing truth behind the messages on a community announcement board.

#12 - Poisoned Land: Savage hunters patrol the Poisoned Lands, demanding appeasement from the three survivors trapped in a surrounded building. How far will each one of them go to survive?

#13 - Pool of Light: A mysterious wave of dark energy from space washes over the Earth, trapping a woman and her friends in pools of light. Beyond the edges of the light, deep pockets of darkness hold much more than just empty blackness.

#14 - Ghosts of Pompeii: A woman on a tour of Italy with her son unwittingly awakens the ghosts of Pompeii.

#15 - Sparklers: A child's sparkler opens a doorway to another dimension and a father must enter it to save his family and his neighborhood from the ominous threat that lays beyond.

#16 - The Grid: An interstellar salvage crew activates a mysterious grid on an abandoned vessel floating in space, unleashing a deadly force.

#17 - The Barn: An empty barn beckons an amateur photographer to step through its dark entrance, whispering promises of a once-in-a-lifetime shoot.

#18 - Sands of the Colosseum: A businessman in Rome gets to experience the dream of a lifetime when he visits the great Colosseum — until he finds himself standing on the arena floor.

#19 - Flipbook: A man sees a dark future of his family in jeopardy when he watches the tiny animations of a flipbook play out in his hand.

#20 - Day of the Hoppers: Two boys flee for their lives when their friendly neighborhood grasshoppers turn into deadly projectiles.

Land of Fright™ terrorstories contained in Collection IV:

#31 - The Throw-Aways: A washed-up writer of action-adventure thrillers is menaced by the ghosts of the characters he has created.

#32 - Everlasting Death: The souls of the newly deceased take on solid form and the Earth fills with immovable statues of death...

#33 - Bite the Bullet: In the Wild West, a desperate outlaw clings to a bullet cursed by a Gypsy... because the bullet has his name on it.

#34 - Road Rage: A senseless accident on a rural highway sets off a frightening chain of events.

#35 - The Controller: A detective investigates a bank robbery that appears to have been carried out by a zombie.

#36 - The Notebook: An enchanted notebook helps a floundering author finish her story. But the unnatural fuel that stokes the power of the mysterious writing journal leads her down a disturbing path...

#37 - The Candy Striper and the Captain: American WWII soldiers in the Philippines scare superstitious enemy soldiers with corpses they dress up to look like vampire victims. The vampire bites might be fake, but what comes out of the jungle is not...

#38 - Clothes Make the Man: A young man steals a magical suit off of a corpse, hoping some of its power will rub off on him.

#39 - Memory Market: The cryptic process of memory storage in the human brain has been decoded and now memories are bought and sold in the memory market. But with every legitimate commercial endeavor there comes a black market, and the memory market is no exception...

#40 - The Demon Who Ate Screams: A young martial artist battles a vicious demon who feeds on the tormented screams and dying whimpers of his victims.

Land of Fright™ terrorstories contained in Collection V:

#41 - The Hatchlings: A peaceful barbecue turns into an afternoon of terror for a suburban man when the charcoal briquets start to hatch!

#42 - Virgin Sacrifice: A professor of archaeology is determined to set the world right again using the ancient power of Aztec sacrifice rituals.

#43 - Smog Monsters: The heavily contaminated air in Beijing turns even deadlier when unearthly creatures form within the dense poison of its thick pollution.

#44 - Benders of Space-Time: A young interstellar traveler discovers the uncomfortable truth about the Benders, the creatures who power starships with their ability to fold space-time.

#45 - The Picture: A young soldier in World War II shows his fellow soldiers a picture of his beautiful fiancé during the lulls in battle. But this seemingly harmless gesture is far from innocent...

#46 - Black Ice: A vicious dragon is offered a great gift — a block of black ice to soothe the fire that burns its throat and roars in its belly. Too bad the dragon has never heard of a Trojan dwarf...

#47 - Artist Alley: At a comic book convention, a seedy comic book publisher sees himself depicted in a disturbing series of artist drawings.

#48 - Dead Zone: A yacht gets caught adrift in the dead zone in the Gulf of Mexico, trapped in an area of the sea that contains no life. What comes aboard the yacht from the depths of this dead zone in search of food cannot really be considered alive...

#49 - Cemetery Dance: A suicidal madman afraid to take his own life attempts to torment a devout Christian man into killing him.

#50 - The King Who Owned the World: A bored barbarian king demands he be brought a new challenger. But who can you find to battle a king who owns the world?

Land of Fright™ terrorstories contained in Collection VI:

#51 - Zombie Carnival: Two couples stumble upon a zombie-themed carnival and decide to join the fun.

#52 - Going Green: Drug runners trying to double cross their boss get a taste of strong voodoo magic.

#53 - Message In A Bottle: A bottle floats onto the beach of a private secluded island with an unnerving message trapped inside.

#54 - The Chase: In 18th century England, a desperate chase is on as a monstrous beast charges after a fleeing wagon, a wagon occupied by too many people...

#55 - Who's Your Daddy?: A lonely schoolteacher is disturbed by how much all of the students in her class look alike. A visit by a mysterious man sheds some light on the curious situation.

#56 - Beheaded: In 14th century England, a daughter vows revenge upon those who beheaded her father. She partners with a lascivious young warlock to restore her family's honor.

#57 - Hold Your Breath: A divorced mother of one confronts the horrible truth behind the myth of holding one's breath when driving past a cemetery.

#58 - Viral: What makes a civilization fall? Volcanoes, earthquakes, or other forces of nature? Barbarous invasions or assaults from hostile forces? Decline from within due to decadence and moral decay? Or could it be something more insidious?

#59 - Top Secret: A special forces agent confronts the villainous characters from his past, but discovers something even more dangerous. Trust.

#60 - Immortals Must Die: There is no more life force left in the universe. The attainment of immortality has depleted the world of available souls. So what do you do if you are desperate to have a child?

AND LOOK FOR EVEN MORE
LAND OF FRIGHT™ TALES
COMING SOON!

THANKS AGAIN FOR READING.

Visit www.landoffright.com

Made in the USA
Las Vegas, NV
06 February 2023

67012178R00163